GHOSTS OF THE UNREMEMBERED PAST

Ghosts of the Unremembered Past

Tom Wooldridge

IPBOOKS.net
International Psychoanalytic Books

Published by IPBooks, Queens, NY 2019
Online at: www.IPBooks.net

Cover Painting by **Christian Krohg** (13 August 1852–16 October 1925) (Sleeping mother with child. 1883)
Typesetting and formatting services by Self-Publishing Lab

ISBN: 978-1-949093-37-7

For my father,
who told me stories
and my analyst,
who helped me learn to tell them.

In every nursery there are ghosts. They are the visitors from the unremembered past of the parents, the uninvited guests at the christening. Under all favorable circumstances the unfriendly and unbidden spirits are banished from the nursery and return to their subterranean dwelling place.... But how shall we explain another group of families who appear to be possessed by their ghosts? The intruders from the past have taken up residence in the nursery, claiming tradition and rights of ownership. They have been present at the christening for two or more generations. While no one has issued an invitation, the ghosts take up residence and conduct the rehearsal of the family tragedy from a tattered script.

—Selma Fraiberg, Edna Adelson and Vivian Shapiro
Ghosts in the Nursery: A Psychoanalytic Approach to the Problems of Impaired Mother-Infant Relationships (1975)

It is to the realm of these bad objects, I feel convinced, rather than to the realm of the super-ego that the ultimate origin of all psychopathological developments is to be traced; for it may be said of all psychoneurotic and psychotic patients that, if a True Mass is being celebrated in the chancel, a Black Mass is being celebrated in the crypt. It becomes evident, accordingly, that the psychotherapist is the true successor to the exorcist, and that he is concerned, not only with "the forgiveness of sins" but also with "the casting out of devils."

—Ronald Fairbairn
Psychoanalytic Studies of the Personality (1952)

PREFACE

Dottie felt a sense of dread building in her stomach as she made her way to the nursery. Her husband, Henry, had brought home an old bassinet one evening a few months ago, in celebration of the couple's expected child. He had held it out for her inspection, though she had turned away immediately, occupied with the business of frying chicken. The offering had made her strangely uncomfortable, as had most of the pregnancy. Her belly had been swollen for near four weeks before she'd told him that she was expecting. Though he had been delighted, hugging her tightly upon hearing the news, she had quickly disentangled from his embrace, revolted by the idea that a child grew inside her. Now that wicker cradle, its inside covered with light blue cloth, held their son, born only days earlier.

This was the first time she had been alone with her son. In the weeks before labor, her husband had brought in help: a middle-aged black woman with a weathered face and hands, the remnants of a youth spent picking cotton. As she lay in bed one afternoon, ripe with her pregnancy, he had come into the bedroom with the woman in tow.

"Dottie, I've brought in help for you."

Her resentment flared. How dare he bring her help now, after she'd been left to struggle these many months, full with child? He had done this to her, after all, and the whole world had been able to see the sinfulness of it in her body, thick and heavy and entirely disgusting. Now, she withdrew further into herself, cloaked in anger.

When she made no response, he continued hopefully, "This old negro woman here is called Hattie. She's had no children of her own, but comes recommended by the Walker family. Practically raised their youngest son, Jack told me. A good Christian woman, too. Her husband's a reverend." Henry rarely spoke at such length and he shifted uncomfortably in the silence that followed his words. That silence was filled with unease.

Standing beside him, hands clasped before her, Hattie looked upon the woman laying in bed, her face swollen and moist, red quilt covering her protruding belly, and said nothing. She had learned from many years of working with white families that it was best for a maid to stay out of the family's affairs. Yes, that only brought pain, for though many white folks suffered from a terrible loneliness and would confide their suffering to a maid, they'd resent her all the while for knowing their secret shame. Careful that her expression not reveal her innermost thoughts, she counseled herself, "This woman here is afflicted. Good Lord, and with a child coming. Sure enough, what I can do here is to offer prayers for that there child, and both these parents, this coming Sunday."

"Dottie, do you hear me?" Henry asked, receiving no response.

She rolled over, grunting as her body protested, and surrendered herself to the darkness of sleep. She never heard Henry finally leave the room, a sigh of resignation on his lips and with Hattie slipping away quietly behind him. Dottie's dreams, as they had been these past months, were fitful, cast with vivid images of her husband making love to other women, his animal lust having overtaken him entirely; or else of her child kicking against her swollen belly, its skin unusually thin and near breaking. Some nights she found herself waking, a scream on her lips, her legs tangled in sheets wet and stinking with stale sweat.

The next few weeks passed slowly as her body ached with discomfort and heaviness. With nothing to occupy her mind, she was left in her waking hours, which increased with her discomfort, awash in dreadful anticipation. What she was waiting for, she didn't know, yet the feeling was familiar—infinitely deep and entirely incomprehensible to her. That feeling had been an incessant accompaniment to life itself.

Weeks later, as she lay in bed recovering from her long and painful labor, she often heard Hattie humming softly to the baby boy and, as she began to move about the house, observed the old woman's tenderness toward the child with growing suspicion. Now, with Hattie away tending to her husband's congregation for the evening, she tentatively picked up her sleeping son and walked over to the nearby rocking chair, a relic of her family's past. According to her mother, the chair had been passed down by three generations of her family's women. Though its cushion had worn out long ago, batting bursting at its edges for as long as she could recall, its frame remained sound. Looking at her son, she frowned.

"You're a skinny, pink little thing, aren't you? Not much good for nothing yet."

The baby giggled and spit, moving in his mother's arms. She sighed and shifted her weight in the chair, still sore from her long labor. She remembered the pain she had felt in that hospital bed and her hatred for the young nurse who was her only company. This, she thought, was the burden of women, inherited from that old transgression in Eden the preacher talked about from time to time. Yes, this was her punishment, which felt entirely deserved and right, for it was the Lord's will. Yet her resentment smoldered.

Occupied with these thoughts, she realized that her son was struggling in her arms, the blankets wrapped around his small body beginning to loosen. Looking down at him, she smiled as she took in his shriveled face, his brown eyes seeming to convey an intelligence that surprised her. The two regarded each other silently for several moments before, to her horror, she discovered that his blankets had fallen away entirely, leaving his penis—small, pink and erect—exposed. With a loud gasp, she jumped from her chair and stumbled over to the bassinet, roughly depositing him inside before rushing out of the room.

When Henry arrived home several hours later, he found the house quiet except for the sound of his son's whimpering. Disturbed by the noise but uncertain about how to comfort the child, he went looking for his wife and found her bedroom door locked.

"Dottie, you in there?" he asked, voice only slightly raised.

He strained to listen, unsure whether he could hear traces of movement inside the room. For several minutes he waited and finally, receiving no response, turned and walked into the living room, reclining in his favorite chair and taking out his pipe. Packing it with tobacco, he smoked, finding relief from an escalating sense of foreboding that had begun to overtake him. For some time, he wondered what he ought to do next before at last putting down his pipe, picking up the old rotary phone next to his chair to summon Hattie and, then, dialing the family doctor, a man whose number he knew all too well.

ONE

Graham sat in the waiting room and shivered. Although the weather outside was mild, his hands were like ice, a feeling that, while uncomfortable, had become as familiar to him as his own heartbeat, which often raced with anxiety. His mind was mostly empty, but his body was tense with anticipation and another feeling that was less discernible. Hope, perhaps; though if you asked him what he hoped for, he wouldn't have been able to say.

He had done well enough in his academic pursuits, graduating with a bachelors degree at a local college and enrolling in a doctoral program in philosophy at a state university on the East Coast, a move that had taken him far from his small family. And yet he had never been able to realize his potential in his studies, often finding himself stuck in loops of thought and feeling that led nowhere. Even more distressing, aside from his high-school girlfriend, he had yet to find himself in a romantic relationship that lasted for more than a few dates. As these relationships progressed, he fled, driven away by the fear and shame that threatened to engulf him.

One afternoon, after a few beers with his graduate advisor at the local pub and his inhibitions loosened, Graham confessed his disappointments: first with a brief, embittered remark about his difficulties with women and then, with his advisor's gentle encouragement, at greater length. He discovered, much to his surprise, that talking brought relief. He was starving to speak with someone about troubles that had been, up to that point, entirely private. His advisor, exuding a kind of fatherly wisdom that Graham had been unable to find in his own father, paused and sipped his beer for a moment before responding.

"You haven't told me much about your life before graduate school," he said, pausing again to stroke his salt-and-pepper beard, "but I know you suffered an early loss. You've told me that much, and I can only imagine that brought its share of difficulties."

"I suppose it did," Graham replied, "but I honestly haven't given much thought as to how. And despite that, I grew up with people who cared about me, that's for sure. But I somehow feel that I've never able to get close to another person, especially a woman. Each time I try, and believe me there haven't been many, the urge to run and hide overtakes me."

Surprised to find that his eyes were wet with tears, he attempted, unsuccessfully, to discretely wipe them away with the back of his palm. "It's ridiculous to still be struggling with these problems at my age, you know? I should have figured this out already." His advisor drummed his fingers on the hardwood table, its surface stained from years of cold, sweating glasses and spilled beer, a thoughtful smile on his face. "It's not easy," he replied finally. "Believe me, I know from my own experience." Several moments of silence passed as both men focused intently on their drinks, each taking a sip from time to time.

"You know, you might consider going into psychoanalysis. It's something that I benefitted from immensely when I was a younger man. I hope this isn't presumptuous, but I think you might, too."

Graham woke up the next morning with a headache and thoroughly embarrassed about his vulnerability the night before. As they had left the bar soon after their conversation, his advisor had pressed a sheet of paper into his palm with two names of "well-respected and competent" psychoanalysts. "Give it some thought," he said, lightly slapping Graham on the back before turning to walk toward the bus that would carry him home.

Although the thought of meeting with a psychoanalyst left him uneasy, that morning he called and asked for an initial appointment. Within a few hours, he found that Dr. Clarice, the first analyst on the list, had called back and offered him a time for an initial consultation.

Now, he looked around the office's waiting area, four straight-backed wooden chairs and a plain coffee table that held a spray of magazines, popular titles that held no interest for him, occupying the otherwise spare room. On the wall hung a single piece of art, a thin black frame holding a line drawing of a mother and baby elephant, the former's tail held by the baby's trunk as the pair walked along. He was impressed by the technical skill of the artist, as counter lines of varying weights had been used to capture the dimensionality of the beasts and somehow—perhaps it was the distance between the lines— even the thickness of the skin on the animals' wrinkled trunks had been represented.

Seeking relief from his anxiety, he picked up a magazine, without concern for its contents, from the table and flipped through it, stopping at an article that began with a striking picture of a hawk, its round black-and-yellow eye staring at the camera. He began to read the piece, making it through several paragraphs before the office door opened. A thin woman, probably in her 60s and professionally dressed in black slacks and a plain white blouse, emerged. "Graham?" she asked with a smile.

He stood and nodded, shaking the woman's hand briefly. Her palm, he noted, was cool and dry, in contrast to his, which was moist with anticipation.

"I'm Dr. Clarice. It's nice to meet you," she said. "This way, please."

Following her instructions, he stepped past her and through the door, walking down a long hall before turning left to enter through another door that opened into a moderately sized office. Within moments, she entered behind him. "Please, take a seat," she said, gesturing with her hand as she sat. He stood for a several seconds longer, looking out through two large windows at the far end of the office into a well-tended garden. A hummingbird feeder dangled from a tree branch, the top of which extended upward and out of sight. The sunlight, so prominent earlier in the day, was now obscured by clouds and it was, he noticed, beginning to rain. The hummingbird feeder swayed with the wind.

He settled into a comfortable, dark brown leather chair and examined the room further. Bookshelves lined the walls behind him, each shelf holding unfamiliar titles. On the wall across from where he sat was an abstract painting, vibrant eruptions of color sweeping across its white canvas. Beneath it was a couch, perhaps six feet long and unlike any he had seen before. Its surface, covered in dark green fabric, was flat save for a round pillow at one end. Several feet behind the pillow was another chair where Dr. Clarice waited, watching him expectantly. Although he couldn't say why, he liked this woman's office. He liked this woman, too. It all felt comfortable, even safe.

As the moment of silence between them lengthened, she finally spoke.

"What brings you in today?" she asked.

"I called you for an appointment at the recommendation of my graduate advisor" Graham replied with a stammer. "I have to say, when

I woke up this morning I almost called again, this time to cancel our appointment. I'm glad I decided to come in, though."

As he spoke, he examined Dr. Clarice's face, which remained warm and interested. Her shoulder length hair was brownish red and her face conveyed a sharp intelligence, yet her eyes were kind, even warm, as she regarded him from across the room.

"You've had a lot of anxiety about meeting me," she replied in an even voice, "and clearly it has taken a lot of courage to make it here today."

"The problem is that I'm not entirely sure what I'm here for," he continued, embarrassed with the admission, "and I'm not entirely sure how this process works. I read some Freud in my undergraduate studies, but that was a long time ago and it didn't make much of an impression on me. And as far as I can remember, what I read didn't say much about the details of the actual psychoanalytic process, so I'll need some help getting started."

In fact, Graham had only read one psychoanalytic work during his undergraduate years, in an introductory anthropology class taken in his first semester, before he had decided to pursue the study of philosophy. At the time, *Totem and Taboo* struck him as a fanciful imagination, a now discredited effort to account for the origins of social life and the psychological bonds that hold men together. Though he had rejected the book almost immediately and, with it, psychoanalysis as a whole, he now recalled that the work had advanced the idea that primal man, at his core, has a desire for sexual relations with close family members. It is only through the law of incest, a recognition that the renunciation of violence must take place for society to survive, that such desires become repressed. Even now, the notion disturbed him. What sort of character decided to become a psychoanalyst? He realized, for the first time, that he feared this woman might lead him astray.

"Try to tell me what's been troubling you." she replied simply.

"I'm never truly at ease with myself or, for that matter, with other people. I'm always waiting for something terrible to happen, but I can't quite say what that terrible thing could be. From the outside, my life is going reasonably well. I've been somewhat successful academically. I mean, I got into a doctoral program. But I don't think I've been able to realize my potential. I waste too much time. More important than that, I haven't had much luck dating, that's for sure, and I think it's because I'm always so anxious, which makes me awkward when I'm meeting new people." He paused and cleared his throat before continuing. "You know, I think I've been afraid my whole life."

"Tell me more about that." she replied, gesturing for him to continue.

He looked at Dr. Clarice, his newfound psychoanalyst, with surprise. Having just outlined his difficulties at some length, he was caught off guard by the brevity of her response. Shouldn't she be able to offer him some insight, given the problems he'd laid out before her? Or, at the very least, provide him with a bit more direction about how to continue? Though he feared being misguided by her words, he ironically also felt deprived by the paucity of her response. She should, he felt, offer more than encouragement for him to continue, for without that he was left feeling uncertain about how best to proceed.

"I'm not sure where to begin," he said, his voice uncertain.

"Well," she said, as she seemed to consider what had been exchanged so far, "you said at the beginning of our conversation that you're always waiting for something terrible to happen, for things to fall apart. Tell me more about that: how it is today, certainly, but also how it's been throughout your life so far. When did it begin?"

With this, his face brightened. "I think I know the answer to that. There was a day in my life when everything changed. When everything fell apart, as you put it."

"That," she said emphatically, "seems very important for us to talk about."

TWO

Everything needed to be in its place. With the rightness of this thought firmly in mind, Graham sat at the foot of his bed and began the painstaking work of rearranging the items on his old bulletin board. He frowned upon noticing that a weathered picture of his grandmother, who he had barely known but whose image he found discarded in the attic one lonely afternoon, wasn't quite right. The photograph's edge wasn't parallel to item on its right, a clipping from *Boys' Life* magazine. He couldn't quite say why this bothered him so much, but it certainly did, and so he removed the tack holding the picture in place and tried to right it.

"Dammit, Henry! I know you're cavorting around town with that hussy woman, don't you dare lie to me one moment longer!" The words drifted up the stairs from the kitchen.

"I don't know what you're talking about, Dottie," came the reply. "Your mind is crazier than a bat out of Hades."

He was practiced in ignoring his parents' quarreling, its impact betrayed only by a slight clenching in his stomach and surplus tension in his slight frame. Remaining focused on the task at hand, he frowned again as he noticed that his work righting the photograph had disturbed an adjacent item on the board, an old bookmark with a bible verse on it. In flowery, black script, it quoted the book of Jeremiah: "For I know the plans I have for you, plans to prosper you and not to harm you, plans to give you hope and a future." It had been a gift from his mother, the only ever bestowed upon him by her, on his fifth birthday.

In years past, he had believed the verse, and in his family's religion, with fierce resolve, but more recently a fissure had split through that once reliable edifice. What had led to this he could not say, but he found himself, again and again, less consoled by these words than in his younger years. Christianity lacked the logical coherence that his mind craved. It contained, quite simply, too many inconsistencies. Even so, he still felt an emotional connection to the religion and desperately hoped that, over time, he would be able to resolve his doubts, perhaps with help from the Lord himself. Every evening, he prayed fervently.

"Graham, get on down here for breakfast," Dottie yelled up the stairs.

With a sigh, he placed the stray scraps of paper back inside an old, weathered shoebox, which he then pushed beneath his bed next to several binders filled with his baseball card collection, neatly sorted by team and year. Baseball was one of the few passions that he shared with his father, Henry. On the weekends, the two would visit the local flea market and pick through the bins full of cards, many for sale at far beneath their value. After having perused the offerings and made their purchases, the two would sit outside on a bench, sharing a slice of freshly baked fudge, and review the cards carefully, looking up each in a catalog and comparing its value to the price they had paid the vendor. Bringing order to the disarray excited him and he treasured the time spent with his father.

When Graham arrived downstairs, he took a seat at the dining room table and waited for his parents, who joined him for breakfast only occasionally. His mother didn't acknowledge his arrival, instead staring across the hall at his father, who sat in his living room recliner. He was absorbed in the television, an old knob-and-dial model that projected a grainy yet discernible image of a basketball game. As he watched the men running back and forth, Henry thought that basketball wasn't the game it used to be. These days, the negroes dominated the game and were so tall that they could put the ball into the basket without much effort. The skill of the game was lost, he reflected, but it wasn't worth walking across the room to change the channel.

At one point in his youth, Henry had driven into Memphis with his friends to see a professional basketball game. Basketball, after all, had not been affected by the war, for many of its players were ineligible for the draft due to their height. He remembered sitting in the stands, watching the men, many only slightly older than he, dribble the ball back and forth. In those days, the "slam dunk" was relatively unknown, as men relied more on their skill in shooting the ball from a distance. He had dreamed, in his moments of fancy, of joining them on the court, of gaining applause from the crowd. In fact, he too had been a fine sportsman, esteemed among his peers on the basketball court, if he did say so himself, and this in turn brought recognition from many of the town's young women. Why he had chosen to marry Dottie, given all the beautiful, God-fearing young women available to him, he would never know. Well, what's done is done, as his mother always said.

Dottie began to experience a familiar feeling of unease as she inspected her husband, who seemed entirely lost in thought. Yes, she knew that soon he would again demand lovemaking, as he called it. It had been almost exactly three weeks since she last performed her marital duties. Over the years, she had become increasingly certain that he was a sexual pervert. Even in better moments between them— attending church together on Sunday mornings, eating the biscuits and ham that she prepared on the weekends or the coconut cake that she baked, after painstakingly breaking coconuts on the back porch—she nursed the suspicion in her mind that something about him was decidedly deranged. She did as she was demanded, albeit with reluctance, for she knew this was biblical, but made sure to carefully choreograph each encounter so that his erotic appetites were encouraged as little as possible. Each time, she felt a profound shame that she couldn't articulate and her resentment toward him grew stronger still, congealing in her chest.

As she looked down at her husband, she was startled by a mixture of mild arousal and deep-seated disgust. She quickly tried to distract herself and, within moments, found herself thinking about the horse her family had owned when she was a child: a dusty, unattractive mare with splotchy skin and a thinning mane. For reasons that had never been clear to her, she had always been terrified of the animal; of its large, seemingly stupid brown eyes and its wet, smacking lips filled with thick, white teeth. On many afternoons, her father insisted that she accompany him to the barn in the backyard to collect eggs. Only once had she tried to resist and she could still remember the sound of his angry bellowing as his neck, covered in thick, dropping fat, shook in outrage. After that, she dutifully complied, though she always found herself trembling with fear and moist with sweat.

Frustrated with her mind's wanderings, she refocused her attention on the present. Yes, she would strengthen her resolve to avoid lovemaking for yet another week. Feeling relieved, she turned and found Graham sitting at the dining room table, a puzzled look on his face. "Morning, son," she mumbled, as she shuffled back into the kitchen and poured scrambled eggs, now covered in a filmy residue of moisture, onto a cracked floral plate before dropping two strips of blackened, crunchy bacon beside them. This she then placed in front of him before sitting at the table across from him with her morning coffee.

He did not entirely understand that his mother was mad. Her "nervous troubles," as the family referred to them, had been woven into the fabric of his life since the day he was born and he could hardly imagine her without her strange moods and eccentric comments. His father often reminded him that it was Graham's job, as a man in the house, to look after her and to refrain from provocation. Why his father felt it necessary to communicate this to him he was uncertain, for throughout his short life he had never expressed anger toward his mother. On the contrary, Graham took great care to comfort her as best he could. Now, he smiled at her and began to eat the food she had prepared, soon taking a sip of orange juice to gain relief from the taste of burnt bacon that filled his mouth. She, in turn, sat across from him and sipped her coffee, black and scorched after having been reheated several times that morning, as she picked at a plate of scrambled eggs.

"What'll you be up to today then?" she asked, conveying a mixture of interest and irritation.

"I'm thinking of heading downtown for a bit," Graham responded as he took a bite of scrambled eggs, "maybe over to the roller skating rink for awhile. It's summer, so they're open during the daytime."

"You be careful there!" she said, her face drawn with anxiety. "I've heard of a number of boys falling in that place and breaking bones. Nobody needs to move that fast, if you ask me. It's not what the good Lord made us to do."

"Don't worry, Mom," he replied, anxious that her worries might lead her to forbid him to leave the house yet again. "I won't go too fast. And maybe I'll stop by Dad's store this morning, too, beforehand."

"Well, that's a fine idea," she replied, distracted from her worries about his safety at the roller skating rink. "You let me know what your father's up to down there. I worry about those office ladies. A man can't be trusted in such an environment, as I've told you many a time before. Nothing good will come of it for this family, mark my word."

A few moments passed as he felt uncertain how to respond. As best he could tell, his father was a fine man who made certain to attend church each week and was devoted to the welfare of his wife and child. Yet his mother's comments, repeated frequently for as long as he could recall, chipped away at this certainty, leaving him feeling confused and frightened that there was a side to his father that he did not know. She finally broke the silence. "Finish up now and put that plate in the sink. Hattie will be here soon and she can look after the dishes." After taking a final bite, he deposited the dishes into the sink, already near overflowing, and made his way back upstairs to prepare for the day.

Dottie's attention returned to her husband, still sitting in the living room, engrossed in the television. As she watched him, she saw that his legs, one crossed over the other, bounced slightly as he stared ahead, seemingly absorbed in the game before him. What was this? she wondered with alarm. Surely he would not disgrace their family's home with so little shame. A feeling of unease gathered in her chest and, without intending to, she looked toward his crotch before violently jerking her gaze away. Filled with outrage, she hissed, "What in the hell is wrong with you? Playing with yourself in this house, right in front of me!" Banging her cup on the dining room table, coffee sloshed out, creating a pool of brown liquid atop its polished surface before, finally, dripping onto the carpet beneath. Henry looked up at his wife, startled and confused, before turning back to the television.

THREE

Several moments passed in silence as Graham paused to gather his thoughts. Throughout their conversation, his eyes had been drawn, again and again, to Dr. Clarice's auburn hair. He wouldn't say that he was attracted to her—not in a romantic sense, certainly, for she was more than twice his age!—but he found that she left him with a warm feeling in his chest. She was, he concluded, someone that he would like to know.

During those same moments, Dr. Clarice allowed her mind to wander. This was the last patient of the day. Yes, she admitted, she had scheduled more appointments than she ought to have done. To be honest, her practice was already full. At the beginning of the year, she had promised herself that she would begin to cut back. She was getting older, after all, and her stamina wasn't what it used to be. But she was still helping her daughter pay off her college loans and this, she reflected now, justified stretching herself a bit. Besides, she felt deeply engaged with Graham. He was intelligent, that much was clear, but she sensed that he was also eager for the kind of relationship that psychoanalysis, at its best, could provide. It was too early to tell for certain, but she was hopeful that something useful would develop.

"What's happening for you right now?" she asked.

He realized that he had become absorbed in his own thoughts. "I'm not sure," he replied, embarrassed at his reverie, "but before I tell you about that important day, I should say something about my parents' personalities. That's important in psychotherapy, right? Let me think about where to begin. My mother had a hard life. I don't know much about her childhood, to be honest, except that she grew up on a farm in the country, that her father kept some animals there. Her mother died before I was born. She hardly talked about it. What I remember most clearly is that she was always fighting with my father, criticizing him for one thing or another. He didn't usually respond. He was, I can say in hindsight, a passive man. It was so long ago and I can't remember all of it clearly...."

"That's okay," Dr. Clarice said reassuringly, "take your time."

"I remember spending hours upstairs in my room, rearranging items on my bulletin board and sorting and cataloguing my baseball card collection in great detail. Searching for some sense of control and order in the midst of their conflict."

"What sorts of things did they fight about?"

"My mother was always afraid of something. My nanny, Hattie, who was with us throughout my childhood and in fact helped my family until only a few years ago and was always good to me, said it was my mother's 'affliction' to be fearful. I guess she was right."

Dr. Clarice shifted in her seat, which made a quiet creaking noise. Graham became aware of the sound of rain beginning to pelt against the window across the room, first lightly and then more forcefully. He had always found the sound of rain comforting.

"What sorts of things was she afraid of?"

"Well, with my father, she always worried that he'd run off with another woman. That's something she'd mention to me almost every morning; that he'd be tempted by someone at work, one of the ladies who came into the store or worked upstairs, or by a family friend he was talking to at church after the sermon was done. She had a saying about this. 'You never know when the devil's gonna take hold of a man, but when he does, it'll be by the groin.' I never knew how to respond. I do think it's influenced how I've developed though."

"I can imagine it felt like quite a burden to hear that," she affirmed, tentatively.

"Yes, I think that it did. I grew up admiring my father, but that got harder to do as time went on. My mother's criticisms probably contributed to that. In fact I think she was afraid that I would turn out like my father or, more accurately, like her imagination of him. Maybe that's part of why I haven't yet had a successful romantic relationship."

"You didn't feel he was someone you could emulate as you developed into a man?"

"For the most part, that's true. We did have some good times together. I remember once.... My mother's sister died—cancer—when I was about five. I didn't know her well, because she lived out in the country on a small farm, a place called Tremont. It was decided that all her belongings would be auctioned off. My father and I drove out there the night before the auction to tidy things up a bit and because he wanted to get a few items for himself—things for doing yard work, I believe. We had gathered them into the trunk of his car when we heard a low growling coming from the bushes. It was late, well after dark, and he grabbed me by the waist and rushed me to the car, slamming the door behind us. We sat there, looking out into the night together and waiting to see what kind of animal might emerge. Near 15 minutes later, out slinks a bobcat. It looks directly at us. I can still remember those black ears, white patch in the center, and its golden eyes."

"A moment," Dr. Clarice smiled, "when the two of you were joined together as father and son, two men out in the country having an adventure together."

"Yes," he laughed in reply. Perhaps, he thought, his worries about Dr. Clarice and psychoanalysis had been misplaced. She seemed easy to talk to, even willing to join him in a moment of levity. "There aren't many memories like that, though. He became even more unavailable later on. And there wasn't anyone else to take his place. At least not until I met my advisor two years ago. He has been a sort of father figure to me."

She reflected on her impression of Graham so far. Though he was in his mid-20s, his tall, slender frame resembled that of an adolescent boy. His face expressed a childlike innocence that, in a man his age, might be described as naive. His eyes, though, cast doubt on this assessment, their depth reflecting that he had borne suffering and attempted, however incompletely, to understand it. She felt a warmth toward him and, at the corners of her mind, found herself imagining that her own son might have had a likeness to him, had he survived. She didn't think of her son often, but found that memories of her loss, and thoughts about what might have been, emerged at the most unexpected times.

"Just now I remembered something that might be important. I haven't thought about this for a long time. Once my father was giving me a bath...I must have been five or six years old. My mother came into the bathroom and saw me in the tub, naked, with my father sitting beside and talking to me and she started to yell. 'Henry, what in the hell are you doing in here with our son?' And then she jerked me out of the tub by my arm, wrapped a towel around me, rushed me into the other room and shut the door. I listened to her scream at my father outside that door for at least an hour. 'You goddamn pervert!' she yelled.

"There were a few moments like that, where she'd fly into a rage. A lot of the time, it had something to do with sex. We both learned to stay away from her when she was having a fit. My father said, 'She's fit to be tied, so you best leave her be until she's calmed down.'"

"You're saying," she asked, "that your father never behaved inappropriately—sexually, I mean—with you?"

"No, not as far as I can remember. I'm pretty certain of that."

"I see. So, it seems, your mother's own anxieties could really shape how she perceived what was happening around her, perhaps especially with you and your father."

"I've never put it like that to myself, but I think you're right. If I'm being honest, though, the problems didn't just have to do with sex. It was more than that."

"What do you have in mind?" she inquired.

"There was another time, when I was quite young, that I was sick." He frowned, an embarrassed look crossing his face. "It's a disturbing memory," he continued. "My parents slept in separate bedrooms, by the way. My mother slept in the master bedroom and my father in a smaller room, directly across from my own. One night I was sick, vomiting pretty regularly, so my father let me sleep in the bed with him. In the middle of the night, I threw up all over myself, but my father didn't wake up. I tried to get his attention but couldn't. In hindsight, I didn't try very hard, but I don't know why."

"Any thoughts about that?"

"I suppose that I didn't want to burden him. He had already been kind to me, offering to let me sleep in his bed. I felt humiliated, really, having thrown up all over myself. At some point in the night, my mother came in and saw what had happened. I remember her standing in the doorframe. She knew that I saw her there, because we made eye contact. But instead of doing anything—getting me out of bed, helping me to clean up—she turned around and walked out of the room. I lay in the bed until my father woke up in the morning."

"You're describing an experience of emotional and physical neglect."

He frowned. "Do you think so?"

"From what you've told me so far," she continued, "your mother was a very troubled woman indeed and your father did very little to shield you from her disturbance."

"When I say all of this out loud, it's hard to deny. My father would never agree with that idea. But I suppose Hattie recognized it. Sometimes when they were fighting, she'd take my hand and we'd go outside and walk through the woods. I'd talk with her about the things I was reading or what was happening at school. Anything at all, really."

"Hattie brought something important into your life: the sense that the company of another person—real emotional connection with them—could help you."

"I loved her. I still do."

FOUR

Hattie jolted awake as the bus pulled to a stop. She had been dreaming, she realized, as she gathered her bags and made her way down the aisle. Dreams weren't good for much, for they kept one bound to the pain that marked the past or, worse, left one thirsting for things that could never be. And yet she couldn't help allowing herself to dwell in the dream's remnants for a few moments longer as she walked the path toward town. She had been immersed in images of the plantation where she'd been raised, of the vast fields of cotton ready for harvest, the bolls cracked and the white fibers opening outward into the morning sun. Of her mother, who looked down at her after a hard day's work with a tired smile, her bright teeth glinting against her dark, dusty skin. Absent from her memories, as always, was her father, a man who had disappeared only days after she had been born.

Well, she mustn't dwell on that, either. Her mother's love had been a blessing, more than enough for a child in such hard times. Even now, her hands ached as she thought of the long hours she had toiled in those fields. At the day's end, they were always bloodied from the labor, the plant's spikes having exacted their revenge for her plunder.

She sighed and rubbed her hands, callused and worn with time. Each day, her mother had rubbed the ache from her shoulders and put healing ointment on her wounded fingers. She had been gone for half a lifetime now, resting up in Heaven with Jesus. Hattie said a silent prayer for her. Her mother's life had been hard—harder, even, than her own—but that was the way of things. You couldn't live for this world alone. You had to keep your eyes on the beyond.

As she neared town, a smile broke on her face in spite of her intention to betray nothing of her innermost feelings to those in the white neighborhoods. Yes, she looked forward to seeing Graham each day. He had begun school some years ago, which had been good for him, but it was summertime now and he was often home for long stretches of time. He was a kind boy and she loved him. But she worried about him, too. He might live in a fine house, in a fine neighborhood, but his mother, Dottie, wasn't right in the head. He didn't show it, but she knew that nothing hurt the young more than a mother whose mind was unsound. She had promised herself that she would do all she could for him.

Without realizing it, she reached inside her wrinkled, leather handbag, running her fingers along the wrapped gift she had tucked away there early that morning. Today was Graham's birthday. The night before, she sat at her dining room table, old newspaper that served as wrapping paper and a pair of scissors nearby, and inspected the gift. She had bought it with her meager savings, accrued over the past several months in anticipation of the occasion. Now she looked upon it with shame: compared to what his parents could provide, the small, wooden train, painted red and blue, seemed hardly worthy of mention. Weighed down by that thought, she set to wrapping the gift as best she could. Though her means were limited, she wanted the boy to know that she cared.

The door opened and her husband, George, stepped inside, a gust of cold air following him, as he returned from tending to his congregation for the evening. This was one of the few nights that she was granted reprieve from attending church events. The entire Sunday, after all, was spent at the chapel, first preparing food for the midday meal before singing hymns and worshiping with the congregation. He had been their reverend for almost 30 years now and, as she well knew, a preacher's wife was expected to be beside her husband nearly all the time. Yet she also needed rest before the week began again. "What're you doin' there, dearest?" George asked, peering at the gift.

"This is for that little boy, Graham, I've been watching over at work."

"Ah, yes," he replied, "He's blessed that you're thinking of him."

He came up behind Hattie and put his hand on her shoulder. He said, "I'm lucky, dear, to have found a woman with a heart as kind as yours." She smiled, her shame lifting. The two were silent for a few moments, then, each comfortable in the other's presence.

She stood, finally, and walked over to the stove, where a low flame had kept that evening's meal warm for her husband. With a large, slotted spoon, she put a helping of black-eyed peas, shucked the night before while she listened to the radio, next to a serving of braised collard greens. Both recipes she had learned from her mother. Yes, the doctor had warned the couple that they needed to watch their sodium, but salt was needed to bring out the greens' flavor. Next to these she set two helpings of day-old cornbread, warmed in a cast iron pan only moments before. With the plate before him, George smiled, gratefully. She remembered her mother's advice, shortly before she had wed the first time. "Nothing," she had insisted, "makes a marriage like a husband with a full belly." By that measure, she thought glancing at his generous midsection, she had done well in her second marriage, if not in the first.

Now, nearing the end of the road, its dusty pavement cracked with age, Hattie saw Henry, the boy's father, walking down the family's driveway toward his car. He waved and she greeted him in return. The car, a green Oldsmobile far too old to be fashionable, sat parked and waiting. Most mornings, she knew, he came outside and turned the car on, giving the heater time to chase away the nighttime chill that lingered on the faux leather seats while he returned to the house to finish his morning coffee and to bid his family goodbye. It was a surprising extravagance for a man who, on the whole, seemed to do without most pleasures.

Today, she paused, noting that the car's engine was silent.

Something, she sensed, was amiss. Nearly every morning, Henry stopped to speak with her, if only briefly, before he left for work. Shortly before Graham's birth, he had sought her out to help with the baby, seeming to recognize, though not saying as much, that his wife also desperately needed care. Since then he had conveyed his thanks through daily pleasantries and the occasional gift, ten or 20 dollars quietly passed to her on holidays with a grateful smile. Today, though, he shut the car's door without a word. Hattie's brow creased with concern, a sense of foreboding gathering in her belly. After the car's engine came to life and then pulled out onto the street and disappeared, a man's voice greeted her.

"Hattie, ma'am, it sure was good to see you at church yesterday."

Startled by the unexpected voice behind her, she turned in alarm, sighing loudly when she recognized Jimmy, a middle-aged black man who cared for the family's yard each week. Carrying a spiraling, green garden hose against his chest, he smiled, revealed a long row of ruined yellow teeth. Her face brightened as she replied, "Well, Jimmy, it was a pleasure to see you, too. We always do miss you when you don't come 'round." Her words were genuine, for she always welcomed lost souls into the flock, happy for the respite they found there. He, she knew, was a man who had traveled a particularly hard road in this life.

"Yes, yes, I aim to be there every week, Mrs. Hattie," he responded, looking down at the grass beneath his feet. "I just ain't been feeling' right these many years, and I'm lookin' to set things straight. Thank you for concern 'bout me." She smiled warmly, briefly placing her hand on his shoulder before turning and walking up the steps to the house.

"Mrs. Hattie!" Jimmy's voice was a quiet hiss behind her. She turned, her eyebrows raised in question. "You look after yourself in there, hear? That woman, she's got the madness on her today. Just this mornin' I found her outside walkin' around in her dressin' gown, carryin' around this here hose, back and forth, back and forth. When I asked her what she was up to, she looked straight through me, didn't see me one bit."

Hattie frowned at Jimmy, her eyes wide with concern. Well, these days came from time to time with Dottie. She would have to face it and put her trust in the Lord to see her through.

Pulling a key from her blouse pocket, she unlocked the door and walked inside. The house was quiet, save for the gentle drip of the kitchen faucet. She would have to ask George to stop by one afternoon this week. The congregation's donations, though generous by the means of its members, were barely enough to manage the church's expenses, leaving little to support their family's day-to-day expenses. George worked as a handyman in his free hours at white businesses and homes around town. He could fix almost any problem you'd be likely to find, as far as mechanical things were concerned.

Hattie sighed, running her fingers across the dining room table, which revealed a coat of dust that had accrued over the weekend. She clicked her tongue at a floral plate still shiny with oil from the morning's breakfast and a cup of black coffee, which seemed to have spilled and was still dripping onto the floor, ruining the already stained beige carpet beneath. Picking these up and walking into the kitchen, she set to work on dishes crusted over from the weekend's neglect. Humming to herself, minutes passed before she became aware of a sound, deeper inside the house and just discernible amidst the noise of running water and dishes clinking. Turning off the tap, she strained to listen more closely.

The sound— a light, almost desperate moaning—seemed to come from the back of the house. Drying her hands and with a worried look, she left the kitchen and followed the trail of noise up the stairs, stepping quietly lest the boards cry out beneath her feet. The sound was coming from the end of the hall, from Dottie's bedroom. Pressing her ear against the door's cold wood, she heard the quiet noises more clearly. It was she, that was for sure. She paused, uncertain what to do; it was always best for colored folks stay out of white people's business. George often teased, "You just don't know how to leave well enough alone." Her heart, he insisted, often led her into situations that her head would have cautioned her against. But she didn't walk back to the kitchen, as he would have advised. Though Dottie was mad, her all-too-real pain moved Hattie's heart. Without further hesitation, she knocked, gently, and receiving no response, pushed the door open and looked inside.

FIVE

"My father told me only a few years ago," Graham said, "that my mother didn't do well during my birth. I don't know any of the details and I haven't asked." He heard a door slam outside the office and the sound of heavy footsteps retreating down the hallway, breaking his train of thought. After pausing briefly to allow the noise to recede, he continued, "He's a private man and I don't want to make him uncomfortable. Though I will say that in recent years he has become more talkative, like he wants me to understand why our family is as it is. Fortunately, a few weeks before my birth he went out and found Hattie. I've always been grateful to him for that. He knew that my mother, and I, needed help."

Without warning, Graham's throat tightened, an unspoken worry suddenly emerging in his mind that their conversation would stall and the pair would be left sitting together in silence. Would he disappoint Dr. Clarice? Would the silence make her uncomfortable? She looked on, her face impassive, reflecting on the tension that had suddenly appeared in her patient. Although his voice had remained relatively neutral, she had observed its subtle tremor as he spoke about his birth. Perhaps, she thought, this topic was more provocative for him than he knew. It could be, she imagined, that he felt responsible for his mother's difficulties in the birth, even for her troubles more generally. Children tended to understand the world in egocentric ways, their minds casting misfortune as their own doing. That childlike logic often persisted into adulthood, bringing tremendous guilt in its wake.

"I've got a picture of her, actually!" Face brightening, he pulled out his wallet, its brown leather scuffed with wear, and produced a small photograph. Standing from his chair, he walked over to where she sat and held out the photo. He stood awkwardly, waiting, cheeks beginning to flush, as she studied the image. The photograph captured Hattie's face from many years past, even before he had known her. She wore a pair of round, brown glasses and a red turtleneck sweater. Her hair was pulled back into a tight bun. Though the image was worn, its colors faded with time, her smile's warmth had not been lost.

"Tell me more about the picture," Dr. Clarice said, a look of interest on her face. As she spoke, she decided not to address the emergence of the picture now, right at the moment when Graham had become acutely anxious. She suspected that he had produced the picture in part as a way to calm himself, to give the pair something concrete to focus on.

He turned, returning to his seat, before replying. "Well, I got it from Hattie's husband. It's from back before I was born, when she lived up north for a period. I'm told that she'd been married before, that her then husband was abusive and that she had to leave the state to escape him. Some time after that she came back and met her second husband, George, who is still a reverend at a local church to this day. All of this I didn't know until some years later, so maybe it's not relevant."

"But it does shape how you see her today. She had been through quite a bit before her relationship with you and had seen her share of hard times."

"Yes, she certainly had. In spite of that difficulty, though, she was always kind to me. Even from a young age, I felt protective toward her. She was black and I was white and though I couldn't really say what that meant—not in a sophisticated way, certainly—I felt that made her vulnerable somehow. I feel self-conscious talking about this, because race relations are such a charged topic these days. Anything you say is likely to draw criticism."

Dr. Clarice had been born on the East Coast, less than an hour's drive from where she lived today. Though she had done her share of traveling, both inside and outside the country, she had never ventured into the deep South. She had, of course, read books and seen movies that depicted the place more or less accurately, or at least she had assumed so. Now, she was surprised that this young man, Graham, had spent the entirety of his childhood there. His voice was without accent, which was puzzling, and he hardly seemed to fit the stereotypes about the place that she'd acquired over the years. At the appropriate time, she decided, she might inquire about his lack of accent, in particular.

Receiving no response from Dr. Clarice, Graham continued. "Up until she died last year, she still told this story about how when I was young, maybe eight, we were out walking one afternoon and came across this guy from school, Dan. He was in a magnolia tree, having climbed up several branches, and looking down at us. He started to say, "Nigger, nigger, nigger." I barely knew what that word meant, but I could tell that she didn't like it. Her face just collapsed as he spoke. I climbed up the tree and pulled Dan down by his shirt, threw him on the ground. I said, 'Don't you ever say that to Hattie, you hear?' And we kept walking. This was totally unlike me. Completely out of character."

"You felt responsible for her, sensing her vulnerability and protecting her. It makes me think of your mother's vulnerability and how you must have known that she was in pain but that there was little you could do to help. With Hattie, though, you had a different experience. You stood up for her and it left the two of you feeling more connected."

"That's right. I was always embarrassed when she told that story. From one point of view, it seems patronizing that a child would stand up for a grown woman, as if she couldn't stand up for herself. But I have to admit that it does give me a sense of pride that even then, with almost no understanding of these issues, I stood up for someone that I cared about."

He paused, pulling a bottle of water from his backpack and taking a short drink. He looked from side to side and noticed that there were several potted plants scattered throughout the room, their leaves a vibrant green. On the rare occasion that he had purchased a plant in an effort to make his apartment more inviting, the leaves had turned brown and fallen off within days. Dr. Clarice, it seemed, had more success, and this reassured him. She could keep things alive, even help them to flourish.

"I don't want to give the impression that I'm naive about the differences between us. I know she must have had feelings that she's never shared with me. Someone in her position, working for my family and probably seen as less of a person because of the color of her skin, at least by some people, should be angry. I don't know if she was angry with me."

She nodded. "You feel guilty," she said, simply.

"Yes, I suppose I do. I remember when I was probably 12, Hattie and her husband, George, had a ceremony to renew their vows. It was at their church, and I was...what do you call it...an usher in the ceremony. I was supposed to help the people who came into the chapel find their seats. And there wasn't a soul there who was white, aside from me. Most of the people were kind to me, but I remember one older woman who wouldn't let me take her arm to help her to her seat. I don't think it would be an exaggeration to say that she looked at me with hate. That made a big impression on me."

"What's your sense of how that felt at the time?"

"It was uncomfortable, but it was also a revelation," he replied softly, "to see that there were people who had experienced the world so differently than I had. I could understand, even then, why she would be mad and I felt that she was justified in it. I think we should feel bad about the ways we've benefitted from her pain, don't you agree?"

"I'm curious about something," Dr. Clarice said without answering the question that had been posed. "You don't have a southern accent—not at all."

"No, I don't. People have always remarked on that since I was very young."

"Your parents do?" she asked inquisitively.

"Oh, yes, most definitely. My mother, in particular, spoke with a southern drawl, with lots of phrases that you'd only hear in the south. My father, well, he was more educated and at times would speak in a more formal way, which I think sounded less southern, but certainly not always. Even so, he hard far more of an accent than I ever did."

"What's your understanding of that?"

"I'm not sure," he replied, puzzled.

"It's quite striking. It makes me wonder whether there was a part of you, when you were growing up, that distinctly *didn't* want to be like your parents. And one way of marking that difference would have been by speaking differently than they did."

"That seems possible. I always thought they sounded stupid, to be honest. I tried to speak more like the characters in the books I read—in terms of word choice and phrasing, I mean—but that doesn't explain how my voice sounds." Graham paused, uncertain about this new idea. Yes, she was right in highlighting his desire to be different from his parents. But could he, as a child, have cultivated a way of speaking that was almost entirely different from theirs without ever realizing, consciously, that he was doing so? The idea startled him, that he might have so little knowledge about his own mind. What else might she see in him that he did not know about himself? The question left him feeling vulnerable and exposed.

SIX

After Henry left for work, Dottie sat in the living room, nursing her resentment. She imagined him at the store, talking with his customers, most of whom were women who passed their days, while their husbands were at work, shopping around town, stopping by in search of new Sunday shoes. They were often young pretty things, in many cases without children of their own. Yes, women like that wouldn't think twice about tearing her family apart should the chance arise for them to satisfy their carnal appetites. And then there were the office ladies who sat above his store, only a short staircase away and frequently coming downstairs on their coffee breaks. One woman, who irritatingly lived only a few houses down the street, had caught her attention when she had last been in the store. Rosie, her own husband having fled and left her with a child near Graham's age, would be eager to find a stable, income earning man to replace him. She imagined Henry's hands on her round hips, his thin frame pressed into hers, hips gyrating, and was filled with self-righteous disgust. He had a weak will, she thought hatefully, and simply couldn't be trusted.

Graham, on the other hand, was still young and, as such, had a degree of innocence. Even from birth, she had fretted that he would grow up to be like his father. Was there a bad seed in him that would eventually destroy his innocence? She wasn't sure, but for now she could, at times, appreciate the quiet, kind and studious boy that he had become. Yes, she would do all she could to keep that bad seed from finding welcoming soil in him. Even now, she worried that the older children at the skating rink would corrupt him, luring him down a path that would only lead to sin.

With a sigh, she stood and made her way to the master bedroom to dress herself. She intended to stop by the local department store that afternoon in search of a dress for next Sunday. Although the idea intimidated her—the demand to socialize with the other women she would inevitably encounter there, leaving her in anticipation of the heavy shame that would encircle her—she knew that her clothes had begun to fray and were in desperate need of replacement. It would be good, too, to get her son to church more often. Many Sundays, she slept through services while Graham and Henry watched baseball together. Well, and stopping by the department store would give her a chance to check on her husband, too. A woman simply couldn't be too careful these days.

She stood in front of the old, dusty mirror in her bedroom and inspected her body. This was a familiar ritual; she had waited through the long, dead weekend for a time when she would not be disturbed. What she was searching for she could not say, yet the mirror seemed to draw her in each time she stood before it, preparing to dress herself. Somehow, the mirror evoked memories of being looked at, of a familiar gaze that although excruciating to experience, beckoned to her like a flame entices a moth. She began with her feet. Examining her cracked heels, she thought on how age had laid waste to her body, which had once been smooth and firm. Even in her youth, though, her feet had been flawed. The smallest toe on her left foot had been broken and was more crooked than sin, as her father had said, and it had been so since childhood, when she had tripped, running through the yard to escape her parents' incessant quarreling.

She frowned and moved on, upward, to her lower legs and then to her thighs. With her stomach churning, she noted their shapely curves, which she usually kept entirely covered. She found their womanliness, their soft vulnerability, nauseating. Her breasts, she observed, were heavy, the effects of gravity and childbearing having taken their toll. Though her husband was always pawing at them, she could scarcely understand their attraction. Her nipples, she thought angrily, seemed like large bruises, dark mottled stains standing in unwelcome contrast to her otherwise pale flesh. She thought of her efforts to feed Graham milk in the hospital, immediately after his birth. The doctor had said that breast milk was the best sustenance for the baby's growing body, but she had resented Graham's hunger, even desperation, as he sucked and smacked noisily, often painfully, at her swollen breasts. Upon returning home, to her infinite relief, she began to feed him formula, which she'd heard on television was just as good.

She moved quickly over her stomach and, swallowing her disgust, forced herself to inspect the space between her legs—that wet, soft place that men, those lustful and base creatures, fervently pursued. She remembered the first time her body bled when she was only a young child of ten. Waking up one morning beside her two sisters, the three huddled close for warmth in their small farmhouse, the fire having burned out long ago, she reached down to feel a sticky wetness between her thighs. Soon after, her mother explained, a look of disgust on her face, that she had reached womanhood and now was liable to commit a new kind of sin, akin to that of Eve in the Garden. Although she hadn't understood at the time, she now knew that her mother had been right. Her childhood forays into masturbation had left her feeling oversexed, an unbalanced creature whose impulses mustn't be her guide.

Now, as she stared into the mirror, a mounting panic began to gather in her chest that, within moments, turned to a disturbing emptiness. She was, it seemed, miles away from her troubling feelings, which brought relief, but that distance also left her feeling unsettled, as if she knew that the reprieve was temporary, that she only stood in the center of a devastating storm. She could not say how much time passed but, slowly, began to hear someone speaking to her. She also heard the sound of moaning, which soon turned to a desperate whimper. Returning to herself, she realized with alarm that the whimper was her own. Sitting on the floor, her head between her knees, she looked up to see Hattie at the door.

"Mrs. Dottie, are you okay, ma'am?" she asked, a puzzled and worried look on her face.

Feeling her entire body awash with shame, Dottie hissed with rage, "Get the hell out of here!" Hattie paused, uncertain, before Dottie struggled to her feet and yelled, loudly this time, "Close that door, goddamn you, woman!" Hattie stepped back in alarm and shut the door, quietly, before returning to the kitchen, her brow creased with concern.

Afire with indignation, Dottie walked to her bed and sat down, stroking the deep red quilt beneath her. It was a wedding gift from Henry's mother, who died only months after the pair had been wed, having long suffered with an unknown illness that left her in near constant pain, her joints swollen and back misshapen. Dottie strained to reflect on what had happened but, each time a thought began to form, an impenetrable blankness engulfed her mind. That blankness was almost intolerable and anger arose to take its place. Yes, that anger felt more certain, more reliable, than the blankness. Moments later, she emerged from her bedroom, again dressed in a yellowed gown. Her lips were drawn in a tight line and her eyes conveyed quiet fury. She approached Hattie, who stood before the sink finishing the morning's dishes, and cleared her throat before beginning to speak.

"Hattie, I'd like you to speak to the black man who looks after the yard. I can't recall his name. Yes, tell him that his services won't be needed here no more. I happen to know that he's been thievin' from us, that he took our green yard hose back to his own house, among other things that he's secreted away over these past few weeks."

Hattie's eyes widened with surprise. Twisting off the faucet, she turned and said, "Mrs. Dottie, I'm sure that Jimmy didn't steal from you and Mr. Henry. Fact is, I saw him at church just yesterday, and he told me he's at work settin' his life a'right. He wouldn't take that hose from your family, that's one thing I'm certain of."

Dottie frowned, her anger turning to rage, though she continued to speak quietly. "Hattie, you go on now and do what I'm tellin' you to. I don't want to have to let go of two negros helpin' me here, especially not when you're of such good use otherwise. Besides, Henry has decided to look after the yard himself." With that, she turned and walked back to the master bedroom, slamming the door behind her and leaving Hattie in stunned silence.

SEVEN

“**I** have to ask,” Graham said. “Where did you grow up?”

“What brings that question to mind?” Dr. Clarice replied evenly.

He was taken aback by her response. It was a simple question, after all, and surely it could be answered without hesitation. Was she deflecting for some reason? Perhaps, he thought, she found him off-putting and had reservations about him getting too close to her. Or had he been inappropriate, asking about her history when he should have remained focused on himself, given that this was a professional relationship? His stomach tightened in fear as the possibilities raced through his mind. In the simplest terms, he worried that he had made her uncomfortable. He absolutely dreaded the feeling of hurting another person, especially a woman who was vulnerable.

“I don’t know,” he replied, “but I guess I want to know whether you can understand what it was like to grow up in the south. I’m sorry if I shouldn’t have asked. I don’t mean to be intrusive. Let me keep telling you about Hattie.”

“Hold on,” she interrupted. “I think something important is happening here. You have the sense that your question might have been intrusive. Let's take a moment and see if we can get a better understanding of what's happening now."

"Well," he replied, his voice uneven with emotion, "you didn't answer, so I took that to mean it wasn't a welcome question."

"It's not an unwelcome question at all. Were we to meet in any other context—on a bus ride across town, say, or as neighbors—it's the kind of question I'd answer without a second thought. But because this is analysis, we're here to understand your mind, to get a sense of why some questions occur to you whereas others don't. And if I respond with a concrete answer, then we foreclose that process of exploration."

"I see," he said. "Do you mean that you won't answer any questions about yourself? That we'd keep meeting, me telling you all of this personal information about myself and that I'd never know more about you?"

"It's inevitable that you'll come to know more about me. Why, even in the time we've met so far, you must have learned quite a bit, though you may not realize just how much information you've taken in. But as far as questions, I tend not to answer those that reveal concrete information that doesn't change. What's far more useful for us," she concluded, "is to find out why you're asking."

"I'm sorry," he replied, "but this is all new to me. You're saying that we could meet for years and I'll never know where you grew up?"

"I don't know whether you'll ever know where I grew up, but for today I think it will be most fruitful to focus on the process that's occurring between us, right now. My sense is that when I didn't answer your question immediately, a lot of feelings came up for you. Perhaps you felt that you were being intrusive—that, somehow, you were making me uncomfortable—and that left you feeling guilty."

"Yes, now that you say it, I do think guilt is a big emotion for me. Whenever I feel I've hurt someone else, or made someone feel uncomfortable, or taken up too much space, the guilt that I feel is immense. It's the worst feeling."

"And perhaps that feeling has its origin in your relationship with your mother. How did she respond to your aggression, as best you can remember?"

"My aggression?" he asked, puzzled. "I never expressed any aggression toward my mother. I suppose that I sensed it could break her or else that she might explode on me. It would have been a dangerous thing to do. Plus, my father always told me that it was my job not to provoke her."

"All of this" Dr. Clarice affirmed, "is important for us to keep attending to as we move forward. You're starting to articulate a pattern in your relationships with women." As she spoke, she thought of Freud's 1914 article, *Remembering, Repeating, and Working Through*. If there were a single article in Freud's corpus that contained the whole of psychoanalysis, she felt that this would be it. There, he argued that what cannot be remembered will inevitably be repeated in action—an idea that since had come to be called the compulsion to repeat. Working through, then, pointed to one of the central and most complex tasks of psychoanalysis: to remember, in great detail, what had until then been repeated in action, with problematic effect on the patient's life. Graham, it seemed to her, feared expressing aggression, in the broadest sense of that word, with women. This, in turn, led him to drastically inhibit himself, or to even flee relationships entirely. Part of their effort together, she now suspected, would be to remember how he had inhibited his aggression, and in fact took on a caretaking role, with his deeply troubled mother.

He sighed. "Okay, I will definitely keep that in mind." He paused, taking a sip from a bottle of water that he drew from his backpack, before continuing. "Well, let's see. Ah, yes. At least on the surface,

Hattie didn't seem to harbor any negative feelings toward me or my family. She was friendly with my father until she passed a couple of years ago. But I suppose there were occasions where she'd come into conflict with my mother. I mean, my mother came into conflict with almost everyone at one time or another." He paused, laughing bitterly. "I can see now that it was often because she made up some crazy fantasy about how she was being mistreated. Sometimes there was a grain of truth to it, but more often not."

Dr. Clarice reflected on what had just transpired. It was, she felt, an important moment between the two of them. He had been able to tolerate talking directly about the anxiety that had arisen in the session, at least briefly, before moving the conversation back to where they had left off. She decided to let him continue in that direction so as to not provoke too much anxiety at such an early phase in their work together. Meanwhile, Graham paused, looking across the room. He noticed a coffee cup on her side table. Its lip was cracked, the defect visible even from his chair several feet away, and the inside of the cup was stained dark brown. His eyes taking in the cup, he remembered, for the first time in many years, his childhood dog, Frank.

When Graham was only five, Henry brought home a tattered brown box, holes cut in the sides, and placed it before him. Looking up from his book, the seventh in the Hardy Boys series entitled *The Secret of the Caves,* he gasped as the box began to rock back and forth, a squealing sound coming from inside. His father, smiling at his son's delight, offered encouragement. "Go ahead, son," he said softly, "open it up."

Graham jumped to his feet and lifted the lid of the box, smiling tentatively as he saw the small, brown puppy inside. "It's for me?" he asked, frightened by his hope.

"It sure is, son," his father replied.

Graham took the dog from the box and sat, holding it in his lap. "Thanks, Dad," he said, "this is the best gift ever!" The puppy, soon to be named Frank after the first of the Hardy Boys, squirmed in Graham's lap, whimpering loudly.

Even now, Graham felt that it *had* been the best gift he'd ever received. His mother had only once acknowledged his birthday with a small party, allowing him to invite his neighborhood friend Bedford over for a piece of pound cake. A single candle burned atop Graham's slice, melting its sugary frosting. While Henry brought a gift home for his son each year, this was a momentous gift, his first pet.

Over the next two years, Frank became his constant companion, accompanying him on his after-school adventures into the woods, or to the neighborhood store to buy, with the spare change his father gave him from time to time, the candy cigarettes that blew out a puff of sugar, and even downtown to his father's store, where Frank would curl up behind the desk at the far end of the room, to the delight of the customers. Finding a small book on dog training in the town library, Graham taught Frank the basics of obedience: how to sit, stay, and heel. Within a few months, they moved on to more complicated maneuvers, including how to roll over, fetch, even to jump rope. Henry was proud to see his son's care for the animal.

But one day, Graham came home to find Frank missing from the yard. He quickly ran around the fence's perimeter, certain that the dog must have found a way to escape, perhaps digging beneath the wooden planks. Seeing no flaw in the enclosure, he rushed inside, fear beginning to overtake him, to find his mother sitting in the living room with a cup of black coffee, her eyes closed but her mouth moving, as if whispering quietly but hurriedly to someone only she could see, a frown on her face.

"Mom," he said hurriedly, "Frank has gone missing. Have you seen him?"

She grunted, eyes flying open. "I never did care for that dirty animal, son."

Confused, he paused. He knew that his mother did not like Frank, for she complained about him loudly, often raging at her husband for his decision to bring the "filthy beast" home, or else cursing that Frank left the front porch covered in dirty paw prints when the ground was moist from rain or morning dew. On one occasion, she had even thrown a coconut—she cracked them on the front steps on the rare occasions she intended to bake a coconut cake—at the animal, striking him on the head and causing him to retreat to the wooden shed at the far end of the lawn.

Now, her response didn't address the question: whether she knew where Frank might have disappeared to. She had, after all, been home with the dog while Graham was at school during the day.

"But Mom, he's not in the back yard. He must have somehow gotten out and I'm really worried about him. Did somebody leave the gate open today?"

"No," she replied, her voice flat. "I told a black man that came 'round today offering to help with fixin' things 'round here that we didn't need no help, but he sure could take that animal out to the country and put him to good use on a farm. Said that he just makes a ruckus 'round here. There, he'll be content."

Graham frowned, tears forming in the corners of his eyes. For a few moments the world seemed to spin and he feared that he would faint. As his vision came back into focus, he turned and ran to his room, tears coming now without restraint.

When Henry arrived home that evening, he found Dottie sitting at the dining room table. Soon after leaving his car, he had noticed that the dog wasn't there to greet him as he walked into the yard, its usual custom.

"Where's Frank?" he asked. Her gaze remained unfocused and she provided no reply. Walking upstairs, he found his son in his room, eyes red and face swollen. "What's wrong, son?" he asked, "And where's Frank?" After 15 minutes of patient encouragement, he finally extracted the story from his son. With a cold fury growing inside him, he returned to the dining room table and sat down across from his wife, her coffee cup growing cold on the table before her.

"Dottie," he asked despairingly, "what in the world have you done?"

Seeming to notice him for the first time, she replied. "I ain't done nothing. Just got rid of that filthy animal that you brought round here. Good riddance, if you ask me."

Clamping his lips tightly, he was silent for several moments. Then, as he stood and to his own surprise, he grabbed Dottie's half-empty coffee cup and threw it at the wall behind her, black liquid spraying onto her already filthy dressing gown, before stalking out of the house and slamming the door. His rage reached its peak as he stomped down the front steps, as his thoughts ventured in a direction that he had no longer allowed them to. Perhaps he should find himself another wife, one like that woman at work, Rosie, who was kind to him and treated him like a man who was important and deserving of respect. Alarmed at his lack of self-control, he chided himself for indulging in such fantasy. No, he must think of the boy and how he would fare alone in the home with Dottie. He must put the boy first.

Graham, hearing the noise, rushed down the stairs to find his mother stained with the coffee, her face without expression. Without a word, he set to picking up the fragments of the coffee cup that littered the floor around her.

Now, he looked up at Dr. Clarice, a solemn frown on his thin lips. She shifted in her seat, wondering where her patient's mind had gone these past few moments. During that time, her back had begun to ache; a malady that she kept at bay, in spite of the substantial risk posed by a profession that involved sitting with little movement throughout the day, through an ongoing commitment to moderate, aerobic exercise. Only two weeks ago, her second husband had gone through a knee replacement surgery. Her involvement in his recovery had intruded upon her time for exercise, a sacrifice she was willing to make given the love between them, but which had exacted its price.

"What's coming up for you now?" she asked, setting these thoughts aside.

"I was just thinking about something from a long time ago," he replied, hesitant to digress into yet another story. "My point is just that my mother found herself in conflict with nearly everyone. Sometimes it seemed like genuine malice on her part—that she *wanted* to hurt the other person— but at others it wasn't so clear. She probably had some sort of mental disorder, a kind of paranoia."

"There is less difference than we commonly think," Dr. Clarice suggested, "between malice and paranoia. We can think of paranoia as malice projected outward. For whatever reason, a person finds it more tolerable to locate their anger in another person, outside of themselves, instead of recognizing it as their own."

"I suppose that makes sense. My mother was a very bitter person. One time she accused Hattie of stealing eggs from the refrigerator. Strangely, she claimed that she stuffed them into her bra at the end of the day to sneak them out the front door. Which is, of course, completely ridiculous. That's what I mean by paranoia. But I suppose she had good reason to be resentful. Hattie, after all, was the mother that my own mother never could be."

EIGHT

The next morning, Henry arrived at work early. His greatest pleasure was to sit in his store before opening and watch the sun fill up the room, illuminating rows of benches and shelves filled with shoes. These moments, he thought gratefully, provided respite that he desperately needed. As he felt the warm sun on his skin, he recalled the incident from that morning. Although he had asked the question of himself many times, he did so yet again: What was wrong with this woman he had married? Something, he reflected, was dreadfully amiss with her. With that thought, his chest began to tighten. In a move that had become habitual over these past years, he now reassured himself that hers were the worries of women, who thought differently than men. Besides, their family was blessed in many ways. The tension in his chest eased and his thoughts turned to work.

The front bell rang. Relieved at the distraction, Henry looked up from reviewing the previous week's receipts and saw his son smiling at him. Graham loved to visit his father's store. The rows of neatly lined shoes, separated by type—women's flats here, men's dress shoes there—satisfied his craving for order and predictability. The quiet, dusty atmosphere soothed his nerves. At home, the walls of his room seemed to push inward, leaving him claustrophobic, whereas at his father's store he could breathe freely.

But most of all he was excited by the office's pneumatic tube: that long, twisting network that snaked through the building's three levels, mysteriously hidden behind the walls. As soon as he had arrived and greeted his father, he walked behind the desk and flipped open the tube's flap, welcoming the whooshing sound of vacuum air that sucked forcefully against his palm. Pulling his hand away, he inspected the pink indentation left behind, more deeply imprinted than the lines that already traversed his palm. He had read once that there were those who practiced an art called chiromancy and claimed that they could foretell your future by studying the lines of your palm. He found the idea laughable, yet he could understand the desire to know how one's life would unfold. He wished, above all, for an end to his incessant anxiety, a feeling that something so intolerable would befall him that he would be annihilated, though he could never say what that might be. Knowing what his future would bring, he mused, might provide a measure of relief.

Graham printed a note onto a nearby piece of paper and placed it into a canister. Then, as he had done many times before, he opened the tube's flap and prepared to place the canister inside. This was the moment he always looked forward to. He wondered why this moment—placing the canister into the tube, only to watch it quickly sucked away by the powerful air pressure—was so compelling to him. After all, he was only sending a message to the office ladies, as his parents called them, wearing their comfortable brown shoes and long, billowing dresses over their wide, maternal hips. These women were always happy to see him, for he brought reprieve from the monotonous activities that filled their days. Perhaps, too, they associated him with his father, who was always kind to them.

Placing the canister in the tube, he sighed as it was pulled away, up into the bowels of the building. Within a few moments, he heard a loud pop and looked up to see that the canister had returned. Surprised at the speed of the response, he retrieved it from the tube, opened it and smiled. Inside there was a note that said, "Good to see you, Graham!" and a shiny, round quarter. A quarter was a tremendous amount of money. Delighted, he brought the coin to his mouth and bit into it. It tasted sharp and metallic and hurt his teeth.

He realized that his father was watching him. As he turned to face him, Henry reached into his pocket and pulled out three pieces of caramel candy—*sucking candy*, as he called it—amidst several pieces of pocket lint, and handed them to his son. "Looks like you didn't get enough breakfast, son," he said as Graham blushed. He unwrapped a candy, self-conscious at the loud crinkling noise the wrapper made, and popped one into his mouth before pulling open his backpack and beginning to arrange his homework—several projects his teachers had assigned to be completed over the summer break, each promising hours of tedium —neatly on his father's desk, as his father returned to sorting shoes.

Absorbed in his work, nearly an hour passed before he was disturbed by the sound of a bell chiming. He looked up and saw a woman—her hair a striking auburn—closing the door behind her and peering inside the store. His father, who knelt before a shelf of women's heels, quickly stood and turned to the door, smiling. "Mrs. Jones, it is a pleasure to see you this morning. How can I help you today?" He was always surprised to see his father interact with customers. His demeanor seemed to brighten, his language more carefully chosen and his face more expressive of warmth. He was a different man.

"It's good to see you. I'm just browsing today, but I'd appreciate seeing any new items that you have in stock this week." Her voice was magnetic and pulled Graham's attention away from his studies until he was entirely focused on her, a strange feeling of warmth flooding his body. She was, he observed, strikingly beautiful. Aside from her arresting hair, she wore a knee-length green dress and her legs, covered in silk stockings, were long and firm. A purse of brown leather was draped over her shoulder and the strap compressed an otherwise shapely bosom. Eyes lingering there, he wondered what it would be like to touch Mrs. Jones' breasts. He imagined them to be soft, perhaps warm, and that he would find a kind of comfort in them that he had never known before.

Without warning, Mrs. Jones turned, a smile on her red lips, and spoke in a voice that conveyed maternal warmth. "You must be Henry's son. I've heard so much about you. Every time I stop by the store, he has something new to tell me about you and he always speaks with such pride. Why, just the other day he told me that he was thinking of getting you a puppy of your very own. You must be quite the young man." The woman laughed loudly and melodiously without any self-consciousness. "Perhaps I shouldn't have said that about the puppy," she admitted. "I hope I didn't give away a surprise your father had planned."

Graham, feeling pinned to his seat, swallowed and stammered, looking down and flipping a page in his mathematics textbook, a blush forming on his cheeks.

"You'd get on well with my daughter. She's the same age as you, I think. We just moved to town from up north a month ago, so you'll be meeting her at school in the fall." Receiving no reply, Mrs. Jones continued. "Her name is Charlotte. She won't have many friends, so I'd appreciate it if you could help to show her the ropes, so to speak."

Mrs. Jones turned back to Henry, who stammered, "I'm sorry Mrs. Jones. Graham can be shy at times. He's still building up his confidence. I know you understand, having a child his age yourself." After a brief pause, he continued, "Now, I'd be happy to show you what we've gotten in stock this week. Some lovely items that I think will be just your style. Only the best for you." With that, he directed her to a nearby shelf on the other side of the store.

Although he had never seen Mrs. Jones before, Graham immediately knew that she was one of the women his mother was concerned about. Over the years, Dottie had spoken innumerable times about the "hussy women" she was convinced frequented the store in an effort to seduce her husband. While Graham had never known whether to believe these stories—surely his father wasn't capable of such duplicity—they left him worried, even sick to his stomach. Now, he could see that the woman's beauty lent her a power that he had never experienced before and that continued to draw him in. Yes, his mother was right to be concerned.

Returning from these thoughts, he looked over to his father, who was speaking quietly with the woman as he pulled a red high-heeled shoe from the shelf. Mrs. Jones, a twinkle in her eye, briefly touched his shoulder and laughed with delight, her bosom bouncing slightly, now freed from her purse's shoulder strap. As Graham watched, he grew increasingly distraught. His father, he thought despairingly, was not the man that he had imagined him to be. Had his mother been right all along? Was his father a "no good scoundrel," a phrase she frequently invoked, a man who shouldn't be trusted, much less emulated, as he developed into a man himself? With tears forming in his eyes, he quickly packed up his books, uncharacteristically shoving them into his backpack with no concern for orderliness, and rushed from the store, the door banging loudly after him as he disappeared onto the street.

NINE

Graham searched the office for a clock. After several moments, he said, "I can't find a clock in here. How much time do we have left?"

"It's behind you," Dr. Clarice replied, "and we have a bit more than half our session—35 minutes—left at this point. What's your sense of why you're thinking about the time now?"

Turning to look behind him and finding the small, digital clock in her line of sight, he replied, "Oh, this is one of those psychoanalytic questions, right? Why am I thinking about the particular issue, the time, right now? Well, I'm not sure. I suppose I'm worried that I won't have enough time to tell you about myself. It seems like one session isn't going to be enough to cover even a single day, much less all of what's going on for me right now."

"Yes, there is certainly a lot for us to talk about," she replied, "and we don't have to, and in fact can't, cover everything today. Just keep doing what you're doing: saying what comes to mind with as little censorship as you can tolerate. That's the process we'll build on over time."

"If I don't get to everything today, I can pick up where we leave off next time we meet. How often, typically, would we meet if we decide to continue this process?"

"That's something that you and I will have to decide together," she replied. "Once a week, minimum, but many patients come two, three, four, or even five times each week, depending on what feels most constructive and fits into their lives at a given time."

"Five times a week!" he exclaimed. "That is a tremendous commitment! I don't see how someone manages to dedicate that much time, not to mention that much money, to a process like this, no matter how valuable it is."

"That's not where most people start," she affirmed, "but some people do come to feel that this process is very much worth that kind of commitment. This is something that we can certainly keep talking about as our work together evolves."

"Okay," he said. "Taking a step back, I think that worrying about the time is a manifestation of this anxiety, this fear, that I've always lived with. I'm waiting for something terrible to happen, some kind of catastrophe that will be my complete undoing, and my mind searches for reasons, stories, to make sense of that feeling. I don't think I'm worried about running out of time per se, but rather I am prey to a deeper fear."

"That," Dr. Clarice affirmed, "is a very important insight. That it's not about the particular worry that you get caught up in, but rather about a deeper, and likely older, fear."

"I know from experience that there are people who largely assume that everything will be okay. They take it for granted, so they don't worry all that much."

"Yes, that's certainly true."

"But how does that happen?" His voice carried a note of desperation.

"Well, some people grow up feeling that they can rely on their parents, that they're loved and understood by them and that their basic needs will be taken care of. If a child has that, especially early in life, they develop more of this feeling you're describing. Call it *basic trust*, the sense that things will be more or less okay and that you'll be able to handle the challenges life throws at you without falling apart. It exists on a continuum."

"That's what I want," he replied, "I would do anything for that feeling."

"And what we'll be doing here," she affirmed, "is building up that basic trust in you."

Graham sighed, feeling hopeful about this possibility, though discouraged that it would take time. "Okay, well, let me get back to that important day. The first thing I did, after having breakfast at home, was to head over to my father's business. I always liked going there. He owned a shoe store—still does, actually—at the center of town. It was part of a large department store, a real institution in the small town where I grew up. Things are different now. There are all the chain stores and my father's little store just can't compete. It's been hard on him, I think. Anyhow, back then I'd go to visit him often, especially in the summer. He was always happy to see me. He kept candy in his pocket that he'd give to me every single time I visited him."

He paused, images of the shoe store as it had been long ago drifting through his mind. He thought about the hours he had spent toying with the store's pneumatic tube—something you didn't see in stores anymore, which was a pity—and about the afternoons spent completing his homework at his father's desk. Sometimes his father would even take him out for lunch, to the small diner across the street where he knew the waitresses by name and they knew his usual order: a slice of ham glazed with Coca-Cola, fried green tomatoes and potato salad. With that, of course, a tall glass of cold sweet tea. Feeling more comfortable in Dr. Clarice's presence, he allowed his reverie to continue for a few moments without interruption, the memories warming his heart.

For the first time in many years, he thought of one of the "office ladies" who worked upstairs. Rosie, who also happened to be his best friend's mother, was the most maternal woman he had ever met. Her bosom seemed to burst out of her white blouse and her hips, wide and curvy, swayed as she walked across the office to retrieve papers from the filing cabinet. When his father was busy with customers, Graham often sat upstairs at an empty table directly behind her, tending to his homework. She was always happy to see him and gave him tight hugs each time he visited. As a child, he had squirmed in her embrace but secretly relished the touch. Each time he breathed in her warm, yeasty smell, he was reminded of the biscuits that Hattie would bake, leaving them out to rise before cooking and storing them for the morning's breakfast. Rosie's hugs, he could see in hindsight, were one of the few times in his childhood that anyone other than Hattie touched him.

"It's so good to see you, sweetheart," she'd say in her warm southern drawl after their embrace. "Are there any girls at school you've got your eye on?"

Reliably uncertain of how to reply, his face would redden.

"That's all right, sweetheart," she would reply, a smile lighting up her face. "You've got plenty of time. You won't have no trouble when the time is right, I can promise you that." Then, with a grin, she continued. "Why, if I were your age, I'd snatch you up myself!"

His face would redden still further.

Now, Graham looked at Dr. Clarice and said, "That morning, one of the most beautiful women I have ever seen came into the store. She seemed to be flirting with my father and, as far as I could tell at the time, he was an equal participant. I'm not quite sure if I understood what was happening correctly. My father has never remarried, and in fact has never dated another woman after my mother, so it doesn't really fit the facts."

"Be that as it may, tell me how it seemed to you at the time."

"As I said, it seemed like the two of them were, or would soon be, romantically involved with each other. Earlier that morning, I think, my mother had asked me to watch my father. Like I told you earlier, she always said that a man can't be trusted around other women. I guess I never really believed her, at least not until that morning. But at the shore store that day, for the first time my father seemed like a man that I didn't fully know."

"Seeing this," she replied evenly, "do you remember how you felt?"

"I felt real despair and anger," he replied emphatically, "and I stormed out of the office. I suppose I felt betrayed, in a sense, like his attention wasn't just focused on our family—me and my mother—and the work that supported us. He also had other interests. When I say it now, it sounds incredibly selfish, but that's how I thought about it then."

"It seems to me that you needed far more attention—not to mention protection from your mother's troubles—from your father than you received. I can imagine discovering that he was interested in another woman, or at least appeared to be, would have left you feeling terribly angry, given all that you had to endure at home, especially in your mother's presence."

"Yes," he admitted, "that may be true, though I didn't think that explicitly at the time."

"Did your father seem to notice or ask why you seemed upset?"

"He must have noticed. I'm certain of it. But we never mentioned it. I don't think he would have ever brought it up on a normal day—it just isn't his style to have conversations like that—but this wasn't a normal day. This was just the beginning."

TEN

Graham dropped his bicycle against the old brick wall, a cloud of dust encircling his legs. Typically careful with his bicycle, at times tormented by the smallest blemishes on its otherwise smooth surfaces, he held tightly to the anger and disappointment from his visit to his father's store. The feelings had followed Graham during his ride across town, his exertion in the afternoon's suffocating humidity granting him no reprieve. With a sigh, he wiped the sweat from his forehead and looked up at a nearby sign. Its red letters stood out even against the sun's glare and beneath them stood a circle of older kids smoking homemade cigarettes, stale smoke floating up above them into the sky. One boy, a black teenager who must have been at least 18, caught his eye, curling his lip into a sneer and speaking loudly.

"Hey boy, you got a penny for a piece of candy?" His voice dripped contempt.

Graham looked up at the teen. His eyes were bone white against his dark, oily skin, their perfection marred by streaks of red. His sneer turned to a menacing grin. Graham stuttered, "No sir, I don't," and, leaving his bike against the wall, walked quickly past the boy and his friends, aware of their gaze upon his back. With the teens muttering behind him, driven by his anger and in spite of the fear in his belly, Graham pushed open the heavy doors of the town Roller Rink, assaulted by the smell of cloying, hot sweat that rushed out to greet him.

Eyes adjusting to the dim lights, he looked directly ahead to the rink's wooden floor, its dull brown surface scarred and pocked by years of use. At its far end he saw a circle of boys gathered who, though wearing skates, remained still, deep in conversation interrupted only by occasional furtive glances toward the rest of the rink's occupants. Taking in the scene with a mixture of confusion and intimidation, Graham reflected on his mother's words from that morning. Until now, he had avoided the Roller Rink, for she had warned him of the injuries visited upon many children who insisted on participating in this most dangerous pastime. One boy, she had told him, was left paralyzed from the neck down and, to this day, received his meals through a tube in his belly and only with the assistance of the older black woman his wealthy family had hired to help.

Startling him out of his reverie, a young woman whisked by, her skates rumbling against the wooden floor. She turned, skating backwards, and looked toward Graham with a wink. His eyes widened with surprise. This, he thought, must be one of those "loose women" that his mother so often warned him against, for he, she argued, would be susceptible to their intoxicating charms by his very nature. The pull he felt toward the girl was magnetic and familiar. Perhaps, he thought as he looked again at her reddish brown hair, this was the daughter of that woman in his father's store.

"Hey son, it's a nickel to skate, plus another nickel to rent."

His thoughts interrupted, he turned toward a man, his skin leathery and hair sparse, who sat behind a counter and regarded him with tired eyes. The man picked up a paper cup and spat into it, depositing the cracked shells of sunflower seeds. Behind him sat rows of roller skates, their dirty brown leather straps a sharp contrast to their bright orange wheels. Walking over to the counter and pointing to the skates, Graham pulled several coins from his pocket and, selecting two shiny nickels, delicately placed them next to the man's paper cup. The man turned in his seat, belching loudly, and took a pair of skates from the shelf, passing them to Graham without a word. Skates in hand, Graham walked toward the nearby benches to prepare. The man's rough voice echoed behind him.

"Son, I reckon you oughtta mind yourself with them there boys. They ain't from the good part of town, you know, and you shouldn't be tanglin' with 'em."

Graham nodded but offered no reply and began strapping on his skates which, he discovered, were several sizes too large. With these tied tight, he rose, haltingly at first with one hand placed on a nearby railing and, later, on a dusty brown wall. He made his way out onto the rink and toward the boys at its far end.

He found that he could maintain his balance if he moved slowly and kept his body upright with the wall always in close reach. Within only a few moments, he moved away from the wall, more confident in his balance as he glided along. Though bookish and not a sportsman, he was not physically incapable, having spent much of his idle time outside, climbing trees and running through the forest.

As he approached the boys at the far end of the rink, one, whose height marked him as the eldest, looked up and, punching a nearby friend on the arm, gestured in Graham's direction with a contemptuous laugh. The boys began to exchange comments between themselves and, moments later, the eldest skated toward Graham, coming to a stop by planting his back foot and allowing his front to trace a circle as he spun before halting, facing him. With the boy now only feet away,

Graham was assaulted by the rank smell of sweat, accreted from several days without washing, emanating from the boy's painfully thin body. Betraying nothing, the older boy smiled.

"This here is our territory, boy. What you think you're doin' round here?"

"It's nice to meet you," Graham replied, nervously extending a hand in greeting.

The boy smacked his large, discolored lips, revealing a single golden tooth amidst a row of small teeth stained light brown. After a momentary pause in which he seemed to make a decision, he looked down contemptuously before slapping Graham's extended hand away with a laugh. Before Graham could respond, without warning both the boy's hands shot out towards his chest, pushing Graham hard. He flew backwards, both skates leaving the floor and his arms waving in a futile effort to regain balance. His back, and then his head, impacted the old wooden floor with a loud crack and, momentarily, his vision went dark.

Stunned by the impact and with tears in his eyes, he was only vaguely aware that the boy had become distracted by events elsewhere in the rink. Gathering his wits, Graham used the wall to pull himself to his feet and, with confusion, noticed that all the boys were looking toward the rink's entrance. He followed their gaze and saw a tall, thin youth walk in, cigarette behind his ear, who soon made a knowing gesture toward the rink's attendant. Dropping a black bag from which he then withdrew a pair of shiny new roller skates, the boy made his way out onto the rink quickly, gliding across the floor with ease.

"That's the Monkey Man," the older boy said with a sense of awe and respect in his voice, having all but forgotten about Graham who stood several feet away, his head pounding as he looked on with equal amazement. The tall, thin boy skated around the perimeter of the rink several times, quickly gaining speed, before pulling a book of matches from his back pocket. Placing a single match in his mouth, he began to bend forward, still moving, until the match neared the floor's surface. With a final twitch, the match contacted the floor and ignited. As the boy righted himself, he drew the cigarette from behind his ear and raised it to the flame. With the cigarette burning, he spit the match against the wall and took a drag—never allowing his speed to diminish throughout the entire maneuver—and blew a ring of smoke.

With the boys entranced in the Monkey Man's fantastical displays, Graham, one hand rubbing his throbbing head and another against the wall in an effort to steady himself, furtively made his way out of the rink. Far worse than his physical pain was the shame that hovered over him like a dark cloud, leaving him desperately wishing to disappear from the place as quickly as possible and never to return. Finally making his way from the rink, he sighed with relief that the boys had not noticed his departure. He unlaced his skates and prepared to return them to the rental counter when he heard a soft, gentle voice behind him.

"I saw what those boys did to you. They're just peckers. Don't worry about them, hear?"

He turned and saw the young woman he had seen skating earlier approaching him with a sad smile on her face, a bottle of Coca-Cola in each hand. Blushing, he replied, "Oh, it's no big deal. I'm used to it by now. I'm just glad that guy distracted them."

Taking a seat next to him, her skates still on, the girl put the bottles down and extended her hand. He took it, awkwardly aware of the warmth of her palms.

"My name's Charlotte. My mother and I moved here about a month ago."

He hesitated. In the back of his mind, his mother's voice warned him to stay away from girls like this. They were from the "other side of the tracks," as she had always said with a contemptuous frown. What would a respectable girl be doing here? Good Christian girls, after all, spent their afternoons volunteering at the church or preparing for the Cotillion ball. And yet something in Graham, a part of him he hadn't encountered before, resisted his mother's words.

Charlotte, he thought, was extending kindness to him and that gesture penetrated the shame that threatened to suffocate him entirely. "It's nice to meet you, Charlotte."

Gratefully taking a Coca-Cola from her, he reached into his pocket and pulled out a small bag of peanuts, half eaten. Holding the bag open, he gestured for her to take some and then withdrew a handful of his own. Both dropped the peanuts, one by one, into their bottles of coke, a shared ritual that they both understood, and began to drink the salty sweet concoction. After several moments of silence in which he struggled for words, she spoke.

"I haven't made any friends since we moved here. I've been coming here every day, because I used to skate a lot in our old town, but the people here aren't that friendly to me. It's been a lonely summer, really. My mom's always out shopping and my dad works late."

Graham allowed himself to look at Charlotte, briefly. Her hair was a beautiful shade of red and her cheeks were covered in freckles. He marveled at the fact that such a striking person would take the time to speak to him—that *never* happened at school or church.

Glancing at the clock behind the rental counter, she stood up in alarm. "I've got to go," she said hurriedly, "because I promised my mom I'd be back to help with the chores this afternoon. I hope I see you here again, Graham. It's been nice to meet you."

With Charlotte gone, he looked back out into the skating rink, where the Monkey Man continued to hold the attention of the other skaters as he performed one outlandish trick after another. As Graham watched, the youth skated around the rink backwards before, finally, leaping into the air and twisting several times, landing on one leg while continuing to skate forward, seemingly all without difficulty. As he continued to move, he once again leaned over and, in a remarkable feat of flexibility, lifted one leg up and over his neck. Straightening his body, he continued to skate, one leg on the floor and the other atop his shoulders.

Graham sighed, grateful that the Monkey Man had appeared to distract the boys and thoroughly impressed by his feats. He dropped his skates at the rental counter and walked to the door, a smile on his face. Outside, it was late afternoon and a cool breeze blew, leaving him feeling refreshed and, for the first time since that morning, hopeful. He noticed with relief that the boys he had encountered when he arrived were no longer there, though the ground was littered with half-smoked cigarettes, some still smoking; an indication that they had only recently departed. As he planned his ride home, it dawned on him that his bicycle, which he had left propped against the building's brick wall, was nowhere to be found.

ELEVEN

"That is quite a story," Dr. Clarice affirmed, "and it captures how painful it could be for you, a relatively young child growing up in that environment. How frightening and lonely it could be. Was bullying a common occurrence in your childhood?"

"Believe it or not," he replied, "it wasn't. For the most part I kept to myself. I had only a few friends and only one who I would describe as a close friend. So I didn't put myself in situations where it could occur all that often."

"I see," she affirmed. "And then we've got this young woman, Charlotte, who showed real kindness to you. You were able to step outside of the notions that your mother had burdened you with and receive the gesture that she offered you."

"Yes, I was. Looking back, it surprises me that I was able to do that. As I've grown up, I've been less and less able to escape, even for a moment, whatever patterns around relationships with women got put in place during my childhood. They are more entrenched now than when I was a child, which is painfully ironic."

He was silent for several moments and allowed his gaze to survey the room around him. On a bookcase, he noticed two small ceramic owls that he had overlooked before, each covered in a pale brown glaze with light blue highlights and other, darker colors accentuating their various features. They sat facing each other, their large, soulful eyes making what seemed to him to be deep emotional contact. He thought of the article he had read in the waiting room less than an hour earlier. Owls were raptors, birds of prey, the same as hawks. Their eyes were larger because they hunted at night, whereas hawks hunted during the day. In spite of their apparent viciousness, he felt drawn to the innocence and vulnerability of the figures. He had always been intimidated by eye contact, finding that it left him feeling both exposed and overwhelmed. In fact, he often found himself looking away from Dr. Clarice's gaze to gather his thoughts. Would the strange, backless couch across from him, which he knew from films and popular culture that patients in psychoanalysis would lie upon as they spoke to their analyst, offer him relief from that burden? At some point, he decided, he would ask her about this. But not today.

"You know," he said, gathering his courage, "I think I should mention one more thing before I move on. Like I said earlier, the woman who was flirting with my father had one remarkable feature. Her hair was the most compelling thing I have ever seen on a woman. And her daughter, Charlotte, who was at the Roller Rink, had the same color hair—auburn. I'll tell you more about her in a moment, but every woman that I've dated—well, only two others—has had that same color hair. At this point, I know that's not a coincidence."

"I also have auburn hair," she replied, a subtle smile on her face.

"Yes, I've noticed that." he said, his face beginning to redden as he looked toward the windows at the far end of the room. "That's a bizarre coincidence. I certainly didn't know you had that color hair before I came here."

"Now that you do know, what are your reactions?"

"Well, it makes me a bit uncomfortable. I mean, I certainly don't have feelings for you, if that's what you're asking. After all, you're nearly twice my age."

Dr. Clarice gave a wry smile. More and more often, she was reminded that her patients, especially those in their 20s and 30s, saw her as an old woman. Yet she didn't feel old, and part of her resisted being de-sexualized because of her age. Throughout most of her 40-year career, she had engaged in many productive explorations with patients of their erotic transference—that is, the sexual fears and longings that they experienced with her—and in this way had helped them to find increased sexual fulfillment in their day-to-day lives. These days, she thought sadly, this material was harder to access. Now, she decided, was too early in treatment to insist on the question. It would come up again.

"I see. What do you make of the fact that so many important women in your life have had auburn hair?" Her voice betrayed nothing of her innermost thoughts.

Looking away once again, he replied. "It's embarrassing to say. Have you ever heard of Konrad Lorenz's studies on geese?"

"It does sound familiar."

"He was an ethologist who worked with geese and discovered *imprinting*. He found that baby geese imprint—bond instinctively—with the first moving object they see within the first few hours of hatching. I know this sounds completely ridiculous...."

"Go ahead," she said reassuringly.

"I think I imprinted on these women, metaphorically of course. I know it sounds insane, but Charlotte was the person I've loved the most in my life so far. Since I never went back to the Roller Rink, I didn't see her again until school began. But the moment we saw each other, even though other kids were all around us, she walked up to me, excited about our reunion. Nobody had ever seemed excited to talk to me before, and especially not in front of other kids. I was a bit of a loser, but she always treated me like I mattered."

"Once again," she commented, "her kindness toward you stands out."

"Yes, it does. We remained friends for a couple of years. I fell in love with her—a crazy, almost obsessive love that left me thinking about her in almost every waking moment. I never thought that she reciprocated the feelings, and of course I was far too embarrassed to ever mention them to her. So I was surprised when, one afternoon as we were sitting under a magnolia tree at the edge of the woods talking about nothing important at all, she leaned over and kissed me on the lips. I thought I was going to explode."

"Her kindness wasn't feigned. More than that, she developed romantic feelings for you."

"Yes, she did. And since we were already friends, I was at least relatively more comfortable with her. I got farther along in my relationship with Charlotte—sexually I mean—than I ever have with any woman since, largely because of that comfort. Now, when I go on a date, I'm so anxious that it's almost impossible to have a good conversation. Well, since I know we don't have that much time left, let me tell you what went on in my relationship with Charlotte and then I'll get back to telling you about the rest of the day I've been describing. The first thing to go wrong was that my mother didn't like her at all."

"What form did that take?"

"Well, they met a few times. The first time we were still friends, and my mother told me as soon as she could get me alone that I'd best keep my distance from her. Charlotte had told my mother that she liked to roller skate. I thought my mother was going to faint. As soon as she left, she said, 'Graham, you got no business with a girl like that. She's just a blowin' and goin', and you don't need no part of it.' She spoke like that—real country. I made the mistake of telling Charlotte what my mother had said and it hurt her terribly."

"What do you think led you to tell her?"

"In hindsight," he sighed, a look of disappointment on his face, "I know that wasn't a smart thing to do. I was so naive and I guess I couldn't hold it in, even though I should've." He sniffed, rubbing his nose briefly, and continued. "After that, my mother started asking about her at every opportunity. For the most part, I learned not to tell her much. I definitely didn't tell her when Charlotte and I became a romantic couple."

Somewhere outside, he heard the sound of a car alarm wailing, a piercing noise that made it difficult to think. Dr. Clarice rose and walked over to a window that was cracked open and shut it, flipping its lock into place. The sound of the rain was muted slightly but still could be heard thumping against the glass and the ground outside. She returned to her seat, smiling. "Please continue," she said with an open-handed gesture.

"After a couple of years, we decided to have sex. Up until that point, we had only kissed and not even very passionately at that. This was my fault, because I was very reserved about sex. She was always eager for us to go further, to try something that was more 'adult.' I finally gave in to the pressure and we arranged to spend time together on a night that her parents would be out to see a film. We started to kiss and I was really enjoying it. Clothes started to come off, mostly at her initiative. As that happened, I started to get more anxious. Paralyzed, even. But I didn't ask her to slow down, because I was ashamed."

"Tell me more about that anxiety and paralysis."

"It's like my body just went cold and stiff. She noticed pretty quickly—we didn't even have our pants off yet, honestly—and stopped. She asked me what was wrong, but I could barely speak. I just lay there for probably five minutes, her holding my hand, until finally I could move again. I was humiliated—I really and truly hated myself in that moment—and I stood up, quickly, and got dressed. I left as fast as possible without saying a word to her. She followed me to the door, asking me to just say something, but I couldn't."

"Some terribly upsetting feelings were coming up for you," she suggested, "and they felt so overwhelming you had to defend against feeling them fully."

"Yes, I think that's true," he said, a puzzled look on his face, "but I have never really been able to make sense of it, not in a way that's satisfying to me."

"Here's a thought that we might consider," she paused, gathering her thoughts. "Earlier when you asked me a question about where I grew up and I didn't answer, you were worried that you had made me uncomfortable. You said that whenever you feel you've hurt someone else, or made them uncomfortable, or taken up too much space, you feel immense guilt. It seemed to be quite a familiar feeling for you, as far as I could tell."

"Yes, it certainly is that." His face remained expectant.

"Perhaps you feel sex has an aggressive aspect. That you might lose control of your desire and that it might overwhelm, even injure, the person that you desire."

"That sounds possible. What makes you say that?"

She took a moment to allow her thoughts to take shape. She thought of Winnicott, the psychoanalyst who had inspired her throughout her training. A pediatrician before he became a psychoanalyst, his theories were cast in playful and creative terms that had captured her imagination. One theory, in particular, suggested that children need to direct their aggression toward their caregivers who, in turn, must survive that aggression by neither crumbling nor retaliating. It was only through this survival that the child could discover that the caregiver had a separate existence, that she would not be destroyed by the child's natural impulses. This developmental achievement laid the groundwork for being able to relate to another person, as an adult, as fully as possible, without fear of having all your feelings.

"Your mother was not someone who could tolerate your aggression, as I mentioned earlier. I think that would have given you the impression that your aggression was very dangerous and had to be kept under wraps at all costs—a toxic aspect of yourself. And here I mean aggression in the broadest sense, being willing to freely express your sexuality with another person, to follow your desires with them, for example."

He paused, his eyes wide and mouth open in surprise. "I think you're right," he said slowly, "because looking back, a big part of fear is that I would hurt my mother somehow, that I would *do* something really bad, though I don't know what."

"Yes," she affirmed, "I think that in most of your relationships, you remain in a compliant position, which prevents you from feeling you've taken up too much space. But in your sexuality, it seems that the feelings become more acute. That makes sense, given that your mother directed so much of her own anxiety toward the sexuality of everyone in the home, yours included. Perhaps she saw male sexuality as destructively aggressive, an out-of-control force that needed to be kept under wraps at all costs."

For several moments, Graham gazed out the window across the room without responding, a contemplative, vaguely troubled, look on his face. Dr. Clarice allowed the silence to deepen, for she sensed that it was important for him to have time to digest this new idea. In the space between them, the only noises were those of the rain falling gently outside the office and his inhalation and exhalation, deep and slow. After several moments he turned, meeting her gaze and nodding slowly. "I think you're right," he said solemnly. "There's so much to think about here. It's overwhelming." For the next several minutes, the pair sat in silence once again.

TWELVE

Hattie stood at the kitchen sink and gathered her courage. She had put off talking with Jimmy long enough, keeping herself occupied with cooking and cleaning throughout the morning and early afternoon. It had taken her awhile to recover from that morning's encounter with Dottie. Yes, her insides had been in knots for hours. She had prayed for relief and guidance about how best to proceed and, in time, her thoughts had become clear. On the one hand, she could leave the whole matter alone, letting the woman fire Jimmy herself if that was what she was determined to do. Or else she could speak to Henry about it, with the hope that he'd talk some sense into his wife. Yet she knew that Dottie could be terribly vindictive and if the madness got ahold of her, who knew what she might do? Hattie needed this job. Over these past months, George's congregation had grown but donations had not. He now had to draw on her income to pay for this or that at the church or, just as often, to help one of the parishioners who had fallen on hard times.

And then there was Graham. If that woman got her mind made up that Hattie wasn't to be trusted, she could forget ever getting to see him again. Though she knew it wasn't a wise thing, she had become attached to the boy. From time to time, she found herself thinking of him as her own child—which immediately led her to reprimand herself for such presumptuousness. Hattie and George had both been heartbroken when the doctor had declared that they couldn't have children of their own. "Barren," he had said, a word that still left her feeling nauseous and had thrown her into grief for weeks. No, she couldn't lose Graham. She had been called to this home to look after him as best she could.

Her mind made up, she put down her wet dishrag. Pouring some lemonade from a large, glass pitcher into a plastic cup—Dottie insisted that the black men who helped in the yard shouldn't be given her fine glassware—Hattie walked to the entryway and opened the old screen door that kept the bugs out, its hinges creaking in protest. She said a silent prayer. "Please, Jesus, show me the way in this."

Squinting in the early afternoon sun and fanning her face as the wet heat assaulted her, she stepped out on to the lawn and looked back and forth for Jimmy. Within moments, she found him on the far side of the yard, kneeling down in a patch of vegetables and pulling weeds from the ground. As she approached, he turned around and looked up at her, wiping sweat from his dusty forehead.

"Hattie," he said, "what brings you out here just this time of day? You could fry a damn egg on the sidewalk." Realizing his mistake, he stammered, "Pardon me, Mrs. Hattie, I didn't mean to speak that way to you. The heat must've got to my head."

Smiling sadly and waving away his apology, she began, "Jimmy, I'm so sorry to have to come out here and speak to you just now. Dottie, as you said this morning, she's got the madness on her today. She's insisted I come out here and tell you that she and Mr. Henry won't be needin' you to work in this here yard no more."

His eyes opened wide, his mouth gaping to expose his yellowed teeth. "What I ever done to that woman, Mrs. Hattie? I always showed up here on time, always worked hard, never given none of them any trouble. What'd I do to deserve this here?"

She sighed, a look of defeated weariness on her face. "You ain't done nothing wrong, Jimmy. Nothin' at all. You come by and see me and George after church on Sunday and I promise you, we'll help you find another spot of work. We'll see to it, I promise." With that, she handed him the cup of lemonade she had brought from the kitchen. "Take this here," she said, "You got to be careful in this afternoon heat." Smiling in resignation, she turned and walked back across the yard as he muttered angrily to himself behind her.

He looked down at the black, wet dirt for several minutes, cursing angrily to himself as he thought of Dottie sitting inside her house while Hattie delivered the news to him. "That bitch," he spat, "she's slicker than owl shit." Tossing his gloves into the dirt, he stood and turned, continuing his tirade. "That damn snake," he said, louder now, "I been out here runnin' all over hell's half acre, and she's in that there house stuck up higher than a light-pole." As his anger turned to rage, he reached into his old cloth bag and rummaged around. Finally finding what he was looking for, he pulled out a small, white cloth doll. It was stained with age and streaked with dirt from being carried around in his bag for as long as he'd could remember. He had gotten it from a woman he'd loved for a spell in his youth.

"I'll show that there woman," Jimmy thought as he stood, gathering his bag and walking toward the house. As he approached, he saw that Hattie still stood outside. That little boy, Graham, had his arms wrapped around her waist and she was talking to him, quietly. Jimmy turned and walked toward the back of the house, making sure that he wasn't noticed. He knelt down against the base of the wall, right near the vent that allowed the air to circulate in the hot, wet summers, keeping away the mildew and rot. He forcefully pried the cover from the vent, snarling as he cut his finger on an exposed nail. "This here," he snarled with his lips curled, "This here is gonna jerk a knot in your tail, you damn woman."

With that, he pulled a single straight pin from the sole pocket on his bag and pressed it straight into the head of the doll. A smile on his face, he gently put the doll into the crawl space beneath the house and replaced the vent. Though he felt a prickle of guilt run up his spine, thinking briefly about what the reverend might say about the sinfulness of voodoo, he pushed those feelings aside as he stood, his knees creaking. He turned and begin to walk down the street, picking up speed as he went. "I still got some time," he thought to himself with satisfaction, "to get some drink before the sun sets."

Arriving in town nearly 30 minutes later and breathing hard from the exertion, Jimmy stepped into the Center Street Saloon, the only bar in town where a black man could find a drink this early in the afternoon. Though segregation had been set aside some time ago, everybody knew that there were some places for blacks and others for whites. To disregard the order of things would only bring trouble onto yourself. Life was hard enough, he thought, without going looking for more pain. Taking a seat at the bar and wiping his dripping brow with a napkin, he gestured toward the bartender—a large black woman whose hard eyes conveyed that she was not to be trifled with.

"Jimmy," she said, her voice deep and guttural, "you got money for a drink? Last time you were in here, you done left without clearin' the balance."

"Of course I do, Miss Rhonda," he replied smoothly and pulled a bill from his pocket. Placing it on the table, he continued. "And like I done told you, I mean to pay that balance off as soon as I get my check. You know you can depend on me to settle it."

"Well then, Jimmy," she said with eyebrows raised. "Since you got money for today, I'll get you a drink. But you best come 'round on Friday to pay off this here balance, you hear?"

He drank with relief, the burn of the liquor filling his throat. Gesturing for another glass, his anger toward Dottie flared. How would he pay off his balance, much less afford to eat and to pay his meager rent, now that he had been let go? This job had been the first sign of hope in a life that had otherwise been afflicted. When Henry hired him, Jimmy had determined to set his life a'right, beginning by attending church on Sunday. Now he'd been let go, he thought resentfully, and for no fault of his own. It was that woman's fevered imagination that led her to get rid of him, and she hadn't even had the courage to do it herself.

"Miss Rhonda," he said, the slightest hint of the liquor coloring his speech, "I tell you what, it's hard to be a man in this here world, much less a colored man. I done tried to set things a'right this week and ain't nothin' good come of it. Sometimes I think the Lord done forgot about me some time ago, yes'm, done forgot to look after me altogether."

"Jimmy," she replied, a look of irritation on her face. "My momma always said, 'You can't make a silk purse out of a sow's ear.'" He frowned, uncertain what the woman meant to imply but suspecting that she felt nothing for his plight. In the corner of the room, a man sat down with a harmonica and began to play, its screech rattling Jimmy's already frayed nerves. He pulled another bill from his pocket—his last— and laid it on the table.

Women, he thought, just lacked sympathy for men. Even his own mother told him he was a "no good scoundrel and a ne'er-do-well" chasing him from their two room shack with a frying pan when he reached 15. "You best get you some work, boy," she'd bellowed in rage, "for you won't be suckin' at my tits no more, you hear?" He'd left without protest, first taking up with a woman he met several nights later in a bar. No longer able to remember her name, he could recall the smell of her, liquor mixed in with the sweetness of a woman, as the two rutted like dogs set loose after years of captivity. Several months later she left him without a goodbye, shacking up with a man who had money, the two leaving for New Orleans where her people were from and, by her account, still lived. He never saw her again after that. He'd carried around that voodoo doll ever since, a gift from her and the only sign that she'd once been with him.

Yes, Jimmy's suffering in this life was due to the corrupt nature of women, he was sure of it. Taking another drink, he thought again of seeing Mrs. Dottie that morning, her curled brown hair bobbing as she stumbled across the yard, still in her dressing gown and carrying that looped, green hose. "You okay, ma'am?" he'd asked, eager to help, yet she'd looked right through him, as if he didn't exist at all. And then she'd turned against him entirely, forcing Hattie—one of the few decent women in this fallen world—to let him go. His voodoo doll wouldn't be near enough, no sir. He needed that woman to look him in the eye and tell her himself why she'd ruined his plans, his hopes, for finally finding a respectable life. Yes, he determined, he would set out to find the woman and look her directly in the eye. He gestured for one last drink—to gather his courage, he told himself—before leaving the bar.

THIRTEEN

Graham sighed, finally, breaking a silence that had lasted for several minutes. "This is all incredibly daunting. It's really a lot to take in." He spoke slowly, his words measured. "I have never thought about sexuality as having an aggressive aspect, but now that you've pointed it out, it seems obvious. Even in the most consensual, respectful kind of sex, you're expressing your *own* desire." He looked up from his hands, awaiting Dr. Clarice's response.

"Yes, that's where trust comes in. In a good sexual relationship, there's enough trust that both partners can allow themselves to be used and to make use of their partner. But for that to be possible, both people need confidence that their partner also cares about them as a person, as someone who genuinely keeps their experience in mind most of the time."

"I never thought of it like that," he replied, "but it does make sense."

"Your mother, though, seems to have thought of sexuality—especially male sexuality—as destructively aggressive, as not being integrated with the genuine care that I just described."

"That is definitely true," he said, reflecting on the idea. "She would often talk about men—even my father—wanting to use women for sex, men as having 'appetites,' as she put it, that they couldn't control. I'm not sure where she got these ideas, whether perhaps something happened to her with my father or even in her own childhood. Like I said, she never spoke about that sort of thing, even to my father I suspect."

"There's a sense, too, that she thought of the women who had sex with these men as having been damaged, soiled in some way."

"In part that's a reflection of the culture that I grew up in. The south, as you probably know, is remarkably conservative. Even though I attended a public school, we were regularly told that 'true love waits' until after marriage. When I was in high school, there was this large sign in the cafeteria and students could go up and sign their name to express their commitment to wait until after marriage to have sex."

"That says a lot. You're describing the climate of the 1950s, even though you grew up two decades later than that."

"I suppose that things changed more slowly there. Even apart from the culture, though, I think that you're right: these worries were clearly exaggerated with my mother. They had a more disturbing tone with her."

"Yes," she said, affirming his conclusion.

"So all this makes sense, but I'm left wondering what I should do about this pattern, now that we understand it. I mean, how do I change how all of this feels in myself?"

"Oh," Dr. Clarice replied, "I don't think we understand it completely yet. On the contrary, we're just starting to put into words a very complex pattern that's been with you for a long time, almost for your entire life. That's going to take quite a bit of time and ongoing reflection, seeing it in one situation and then another."

In the silence that grew between them, she reflected on an article she had read the day before during an unexpectedly free hour. Receiving a late cancellation, she had made herself a cup of tea and picked up a journal from a stack beside her chair, searching for something of interest. After reading several abstracts, she settled on an article by an esteemed colleague on the topic of maternal aggression. She spent the hour thoroughly engaged, even surprised when her next patient arrived. The article, she now remembered, referenced Freud's distinction between *word presentations* and *thing presentations*. Although she hadn't been inspired by Freud during her training, over the years, as she noticed again and again the tremendous depth of his insight, her respect for him had grown. Yes, his personality was complicated, rendering him myopic in many ways both in his relationships and in his theorizing. Some of his theories seemed, in hindsight, outlandish. Yet on the whole, Dr. Clarice admired Freud's character and his insight tremendously.

Thing presentation, she reminded herself, was the term Freud used to refer to a non-linguistic, largely imagistic, mental representation of objects characteristic of the unconscious mind. In the conscious mind, they are always paired with word presentations—in other words, with verbal stimuli. Graham's conscious mind, she could see, knew about the difficulties he had suffered and was able to describe them, often quite articulately. But she suspected that another part of his personality had shut down in the face of such overwhelm and had repressed, using Freud's language, a thing presentation, a mental representation of his mother associated with tremendous anxiety and complex feeling. Over time, as Freud insightfully recognized, the anxiety had swallowed up all the other feelings, leaving Graham with an ongoing sense of dread, a feeling that something bad could happen at any moment but with no words to describe what that might be. Their task, according to this model, would be to return to Graham's original feelings, either as they showed up in his memories or in the present, in the relationship between them, analyst and analysand.

Graham spoke, finally, his voice rough with emotion. "This is the first time I've felt like I might be able to get some relief. I guess I've developed a kind of resignation, you know? That I'll never have a successful relationship with a woman, that's just my lot in this life."

"I don't believe that," she said firmly.

"That's good to hear. You know, I guess I should tell you—man, this is embarrassing—that I've never been intimate with a woman. It's not just that things didn't work with Charlotte. That's actually as far as it's ever gone for me. It's humiliating. Here I am, a grown man, a graduate student, and I've never had sex."

Graham thought of the last time he saw Charlotte. Nearly three years before her death, he had driven home from college to visit Hattie, who was hospitalized with recently diagnosed cancer. He remembered walking into the hospital and taking the elevator to the third floor. Long before he reached her room, he saw a cluster of people spilling out into the hallway—all black, he immediately noticed—outside of a particular room. As he walked on, he saw George standing in their midst. Looking more closely, he saw that all of their eyes were closed and he realized that George was leading them in prayer.

He stopped, waiting for the prayer to finish. When George opened his eyes, he immediately met Graham's gaze, as if he'd known he was there all along. A smile on his face, he pushed through the crowd and embraced the boy, now a man, tightly. Graham was surprised by the frailness of the man who had, only a few years ago, still been robust and strong. Now, his limbs were thin and his belly no longer hung out over his belt. Graham smiled when he realized that George still wore the same cologne, a pleasant smell that he had never been able to place. Stepping back, George smiled again before he spoke.

"Oh, son," he said, a tear in his eye, "she'll be so glad to see you. She's got this idea in her head to refuse treatment. We were at a church conference last month, and one of the pastors there told her that she'd be healed by Jesus. But you know, son, I think Jesus heals in all sorts of ways. He uses whatever tools are available, and treatment is one of them, I'm hopin' that when she gets a good look at you, she'll change her mind."

With that, he gestured toward the room, a path through the crowd now visible. Graham took a deep breath and headed into the room, surprised at his nervousness. Hattie was in the bed, asleep. He was startled to see her sunken cheeks, her frail arms. He pulled up a chair beside her bed and sat, entirely unaware of the time passing. Finally, Hattie awoke and looked over at him, her eyes wide with surprise.

"Oh, baby, it's so good to see you. I knew Jesus would bring you here."

"Hattie," he replied, beginning to cry, "I missed you so much. I'm so sorry you're sick. George told me you weren't going to get treatment for the cancer."

"Oh, baby, I'm gettin' ready to go up in the great blue sky. I'll be there with the good Lord, flyin'. Don't you worry about me, you hear?"

"Oh, Hattie," he replied, a sob escaping in spite of his efforts to remain composed, "we can't lose you. We just can't. Promise me you'll take the medicine, okay?"

"Oh, darlin'," she paused for a moment before speaking again. "If that's what you want me to do, I'll do it, yes I will."

He reached over and took her hand and, together, the two sat quietly as she dozed, waking from time to time and mumbling words he could not understand. Her hands were still familiar to him, the palms rough and the tops moist from the lotion that she had applied several times each day for as long as he'd known her.

After an hour had passed, George stepped inside the room and stood quietly beside Graham's chair. Though he had aged tremendously, he was still impeccably dressed in a black suit, a purple tie with a fat, round knot at his neck and a purple pocket square in the front pocket of his jacket. His black dress shoes shone in the afternoon light filtering through the room's window. Finally he put his hand on Graham's shoulder and spoke quietly.

"What'd she say, son?"

"She said she'll take the medicine."

"Thank you, son," he replied, his voice filled with gratitude.

She did take the medicine and the doctors later told him that it had likely extended her life by several years. Three years from that first visit in the hospital, though, she died. Even now, Graham remembered the sound of his father's voice on the telephone. "Son," he'd said, "I have some terrible news. Hattie has passed. You'll be needin' to come on home then." Though it was already late afternoon, Graham immediately began the several hour drive home, arriving late in the evening, though his father was still awake, waiting for him to arrive. That next morning, he went to visit George, who let him know that the homegoing ceremony would occur the following day at his church, led by a friend, a reverend, for he himself was too stricken with grief to take up that role.

The next day, Graham stood in the church, clothed in a suit and tie he had bought the day before, amidst a sea of black faces. He would always remember Hattie's face from that day, its expression now frozen by the embalmer in a permanent repose as she lay in her casket. In the last year of her life, she had lost much of the weight she had carried throughout her adulthood as her body was ravaged by the cancer. He wondered whether she had been in much pain and, though he had spoken with her by phone every month, he felt guilty for not traveling home more often to visit her. During the homegoing ceremony, he had, he still remembered with shame, been entirely unable to cry.

As he stood next to George in the sanctuary's first pew, Graham listened to the preacher, a man from a church in a nearby town, speak at length about how death released Hattie from the captivity of this life, freeing her to rest up in Heaven with the Lord. In a gravelly but enthusiastic voice, he quoted Corinthians: "Death is swallowed up in victory. Where, O death, is your victory? Where, O death, is your sting?" He said that Hattie had left behind a husband, George, and a congregation—a "larger family"—who would mourn her in the days and years to come. Although the couple had no children, the reverend mentioned Graham by name, nodding toward him in the front row. All of the faces turned to look at him curiously, making him acutely aware of his whiteness.

After the ceremony concluded, everyone began to filter out of the sanctuary to the adjacent building where the wake would be held. He walked there with George, who blotted at his eyes with a crisp white handkerchief. As Graham entered the building, he was assailed by the aroma of food and immediately saw a long table covered with dishes, pots and pans. Throughout the large room, people stood talking, even smiling and laughing. He heard a man to his left recounting a story of the time Hattie had given him money when he was out of work; she had even let him sleep for a few nights in that very room until he could get back on his feet. Soon, people started to approach Graham, each telling him that Hattie had talked about him incessantly and that she had loved him more than a child of her own.

As the stream of people began to ebb, he noticed a white face standing near the door that he, himself, had entered an hour before. Though he had not seen her since leaving for college almost four years before, her long, auburn hair remained unchanged, though her face had become thinner, her lips fuller. She was still, he thought, strikingly beautiful. He went to her, a hesitant smile on his face, and then he spoke.

"Charlotte."

"Graham," she replied nervously, "I'm so sorry for your loss. I remember how much Hattie meant to you and as soon as I heard, I determined to come to the funeral."

"I appreciate that," he replied. "It's a real kind thing of you to do."

The two had gone out to dinner after that, reminiscing about old times. Between bites of chicken fingers and sips of iced tea, he learned that Charlotte had never left the town, that she had become a school teacher. Her mother, she said sadly, had died the year before after a long struggle with breast cancer. Charlotte seemed eager to learn about Graham's studies and life outside of the town and insisted that he tell her as much as he could. As the two finished their meals, she spoke, hesitantly.

"Graham," she said quietly, "why'd you run out that night?"

His face reddened. "I'm sorry," he said, "I was just too embarrassed."

"But you avoided me at school after that. You looked at me like I had the plague or somethin'. Like you didn't want nothin' to do with me at all."

"It wasn't you, Charlotte," he said, his voice insistent. "It was me."

As the two left the restaurant, he walked Charlotte to her car, as his father had instructed him he should always do with women. A warmth had developed between them that evening, a warmth that he had not felt since the two had dated when they were children. As they stood beneath the flickering streetlights in the parking lot, her black funeral dress moving slightly in the breeze, he thought she was the most beautiful woman he had ever seen. To his surprise, she stepped forward and, standing on her toes, kissed him lightly on the lips before turning away to get into her car. Rolling down the window, she spoke one last time. "Call me sometime, okay?" With that, she drove down the street and disappeared.

He had not, he now thought to himself angrily, ever called her. In fact, he had not seen Charlotte since that day, nearly two years ago. He was ashamed and furious at himself for letting the opportunity pass him by. While he had picked up the phone on more than one occasion, having gotten Charlotte's phone number from the phone book before he had returned to school, he hesitated each time before putting the phone back in its cradle, and each time he had given himself a different reason. He was too busy with his studies. He would reach out to her next time he visited home. But, he now admitted to himself, he had simply been scared. He was starting to understand what he was scared of for the first time in his life, thanks to his conversation with Dr. Clarice.

"Well, let me keep going," he said, eager to move the topic away from sex. "The next part of the story might be hard for someone who grew up here to understand. In the south, especially in a small town, we spent so much of our time outdoors, exploring the woods, the fields, whatever was around us. It wasn't like today, where parents keep constant track of their kids and shuttle them from one activity to another. Back then, we had almost no parental supervision. I was free to roam as I liked."

"Yes, I can encompass that idea," she agreed, "but did you feel that your parents kept you in mind throughout the day? Did they, for example, ask about what you'd done during the day in the evening, when you were together again?"

"No, not for the most part. My father did from time to time. And on the weekends he would often accompany me on long hikes out into the woods. He would tell me about his own experiences camping as a boy, about how much he loved to sleep under the stars, a crackling fire nearby. But he only took me camping once. I was about four years old and I can still remember it vividly, even though I don't remember that much from then. My father drove us out into the country in his green Oldsmobile—several hours at least. And then we hiked, backpacks on, down a long trail that he said he'd visited in his childhood."

Graham coughed. Pausing, he took a drink from his bottle and allowed his throat a moment to rest. "Sorry. We stayed two nights and it was amazing. My father showed me how to pitch a tent, how to build a campfire. We roasted marshmallows on coat hangers in the evenings and he pointed out different constellations of stars. It was, to be honest, one of the best moments of my childhood, spending that time together in the woods."

"Exactly the kind of time a son would hope to spend with his father."

"Yes, but it all went to hell when we got back home. My mother had a breakdown while we were away and had been taken to the hospital. Since we didn't have a phone, nobody was able to reach us. She claimed that a black man had broken into the house while we were away and tried to rape her. A neighbor found her walking down the street in her dressing gown, early the first morning after we'd left. Even at the time, we were certain that this was all in her imagination. There were no signs of break-in at the house."

"Yet it's such a disturbing imagination. It must have been utterly disorienting for you."

"Yes, I think it was confusing. I couldn't really take it in at the time."

"But on another level, you must have felt terribly guilty for going camping and leaving your mother at home and, on the other hand, angry with your mother for spoiling your time with your father. It would have been a complicated feeling."

"Yes. And my father and I never went camping again, aside from once starting a campfire in our backyard in the evening. He said that he couldn't leave my mother alone, that it was a sacrifice we all had to make given her 'nervous troubles.' And then, later in my childhood, he spent most of his evenings gambling and didn't get home until late. He didn't really recover from that until I was in college and now it's too late for us, I suppose."

"That's a sad thought," she emphasized.

"Yes, it is." he said. The two paused for several moments, letting the feeling sink in. "Well, as I was saying, there was almost no parental supervision when I was out during the daytime, sometimes by myself and at other times with my friend, Bedford."

"It's not just that there was no supervision," she added. "It was that you could disappear from both your parents minds almost entirely for as much as a whole day, perhaps even longer that that. They were so deeply preoccupied with their own troubles."

"Yes, both were deeply caught up in their own ways. To be fair, though, what I'm about to describe probably would have happened whether they had me in mind or not. It was completely unexpected—there was simply no way to anticipate that it would happen."

FOURTEEN

"Hey, Graham!"

Graham looked up, his face streaked with dust and sweat from the long walk home. He smiled as he recognized Bedford sitting in the branches of a large Magnolia trees across the street on his front lawn and looking down at him. Though he was a grade above Graham in school, Bedford, who only lived three houses down the street, had become one of his closest companions. On most summer days, the boys explored the nearby woods and fields, building forts out of broken branches and pine straw, practicing with Bedford's bow-and-arrow or, when the humidity became too oppressive, retreating to his basement to read comic books and drink his mother's cool, if overly sweet, lemonade.

"Let's head out to the fort, Graham!" Bedford exclaimed happily, a smile on his face.

Running up his driveway and opening the front door, Bedford yelled to his mother that he was going into the woods with Graham and would return before evening. Though Graham heard her voice call out in reply, he could not make out her words. As Bedford joined him once more at the foot of the driveway, his mother, Mrs. Rosie, appeared in the front door, her wide hips nearly taking up its entire frame. Beckoning her son back to the door, she pressed two small, brown sacks, likely holding afternoon snacks, into his hands before waving the boys on their way.

As they walked into the woods, their feet crunching the pine straw beneath their feet, neither boy spoke but, instead, appreciated that the other provided relief from the loneliness of long summer days. After a few moments, Graham broke the silence.

"Did you hear about this new girl in town? Her name's Charlotte. I met her at the Roller Rink just this mornin'"

"I ain't heard nothin' about that," he replied, giving his friend a quizzical look.

"She's got this reddish brown hair. It looks real nice."

"It sure sounds to me," he replied, "like you've got some feelin's for her. Next time you see her at the Roller Rink, you oughtta ask her to the movies on Friday night."

"Bedford," Graham replied dryly, "I don't have a snowball's chance in hell of her going with me. You should see her, she's just fine."

"If you say so," he responded. The boys walked on for a few moments in silence. "Tell me," he continued, a grin splitting his face, "does she wear those over-the-shoulder boulder holders yet?"

Graham sighed. His friend was several years older and far more knowledgeable in the ways of women. On many occasions, he tried to join in with Bedford's friendly banter in spite of it leaving him feeling vaguely dirty afterwards. But there was something about Charlotte that was special and shouldn't be disrespected with such crass talk. This time, he kept his silence as they approached a clearing in the woods where they had begun to build a fort—to his surprise, still standing— several days before. Without a word passing between them, Bedford crawled inside while he set to work, using his small red hatchet to split a tree branch that would further strengthen the fort's structure. The boys worked for nearly an hour without comment, sweat dripping down their brows.

"Hey, boy!"

Graham jumped in alarm as a voice—a snarl, really—came from behind him. He turned to see a man, his eyes menacing, coming towards him from the other side of the clearing. The man's speed was impaired by his lurching gait and seeming difficulties with balance.

"Bedford," Graham hissed, "get out here right this minute!"

"What's that?" Bedford asked, his head emerging from the fort's door.

"There's a man coming!"

Standing up outside the fort, he looked across the field. "Sweet Jesus, that's Mr. Ames!" he shouted. "Run, Graham!"

The two rushed away from the fort toward the nearby woods. Graham's mind raced as he pumped his legs. Though he had never seen Mr. Ames before, Bedford's voice had been filled with fear. And there was something terrifying about the man's eyes—a wild fury with no concern for its consequences. Within moments, the boys reached the tree line and, standing behind a large pine tree, peered out into the field. The man continued walking forward, occasionally stumbling on his path toward the fort. When he finally stopped, it was difficult to discern his exact activities. He seemed to be kneeling at its entrance, searching through the boys' possessions. Soon he stood, holding Graham's small, red-bladed hatchet in his hands. He kicked the fort, hard, its structure collapsing as he stumbled backward. Righting himself, he began to lurch, and then to jog, towards the nearby woods and the boys sheltered within them.

Alarmed, the pair turned to run deeper into the woods, hoping to escape his pursuit.

"Let's head toward the train tracks!" Bedford cried.

Nodding but too winded to reply, Graham continued to run, thorns and bramble cutting through his already filthy jeans as he made his way through the trees. In his haste, he stepped directly into a hole in the forest floor, causing him to fall forward. He struggled to extract his foot from the hole. "Shit," he thought, "that's a rabbit burrow!" Bedford, realizing that his friend was no longer beside him, turned and ran back, helping Graham to pull his foot free and to stand.

"My ankle hurts like hell," Graham cursed, his face contorting in pain.

With his arm around Bedford's shoulder, the pair made their way, more slowly now, out of the woods and toward the nearby train tracks. The tracks, which brought the train right through the center of town and out either side, had been an ongoing source of entertainment for the boys that summer. They had often enjoyed leaving pennies there before the train came, marveling at the flattened pieces of copper that resulted. Now they stepped over the tracks toward the trestle bridge, which ran over a marsh that had dried up long ago. Beneath the bridge, amidst the tall, dead grass was an ideal place to hide until Mr. Ames was long gone. He wouldn't see them unless he came down into the grass himself.

As Bedford lowered him to the ground, Graham cringed in pain. His ankle continued to throb and, as he attempted to stand, he quickly discovered that it still could not support his weight.

"Let's just wait it out here," Bedford insisted, noticing his friend's pain.

The two sat for several minutes, silent with anticipation. Right as it began to seem that Mr. Ames had not followed them, the man's snarl rang out once again.

"Boys, come on out here!"

Bedford's eyes widened and he placed his finger against his lips, signaling Graham not to respond. Slowly he made his way up the side of the marsh in spite of Graham hissing in protest and peered out, careful to make sure that he was hidden by the wall of dirt in front of him. Mr. Ames stumbled back and forth near the tracks, swinging Graham's red hatchet in one hand and a half-empty bottle in the other. His face was red with the heat and with his anger beneath several days of his unshaved beard. Even from several feet away, Graham could smell the liquor that sloshed out onto the ground as the man stumbled.

"I'm gonna find you boys," he continued, his voice more slurred now.

As he continued to lurch back and forth, though, Mr. Ames seemed to lose focus on his intention to find the boys, instead becoming absorbed in disjointed conversation with himself. Bedford strained to make out the man's words while remaining hidden from view.

"That goddamn bitch, she's been lyin' to me" he muttered. "She's been lyin' like a no-legged dog. Off she went and took up with that no-good man."

In spite of his fear, a smile crept across Bedford's face. He had never heard such colorful profanity before, not even from his father who, before he deserted the family several years ago, would occasionally become enraged at one thing or another—him or his mother, often enough—after several beers in the evening. But his father's rage found expression in a contemptuous silence that, on the worst evenings, exploded into violence.

As time passed, Mr. Ames increasingly struggled to maintain his balance. Several times, as he walked back and forth, he stumbled, once falling to his knees and mumbling other phrases that Bedford had never encountered before. "God's bones," he cursed, "And Jesus Christ on a goddamn crutch." Each time he fell, he took a long swig from the bottle, now nearly empty of the brown liquid inside. In the distance, the train's horn blared. "Damn it all to hell," he grumbled as he fell once again, this time directly onto the tracks. "Damn it straight to hell," he said, less forcefully and with a long sigh, before he lay back on the tracks, groaning loudly. Within moments, he began to snore.

"Jesus!" Bedford hissed to Graham, his eyes wide. "What do we do?"

Graham pulled himself up the hill, his shirt growing wet against the damp soil. Careful not to place his weight on his ankle, he finally reached the top and looked out to see Mr. Ames lying across the rails. The train's horn sounded once again, this time closer. Both boys looked on, paralyzed with uncertainty. Several moments passed before Graham spoke.

"We've gotta do something!"

"What?" Bedford asked, frustrated. "What can we do?"

Now the train could be seen in the distance, its horn growing louder and the nearby ground beginning to rumble. Graham could see the conductor in the train's cab, his eyes wide and his mouth open, yelling something that could not be heard over the noise. The horn blew louder and louder, and the train's brakes began to screech. In the final moments, both boys turned away, unable to look, as the train rushed over Mr. Ames' unconscious body and continued into the distance before, finally, pulling to a stop.

"We gotta get out of here right now!" Graham yelled.

"I'm gonna see it first," Bedford said excitedly.

Before Graham could reply, Bedford scrambled out of the marsh and ran toward the tracks, looking down at the man's destroyed body. After several moments, he turned to look at Graham, an unreadable expression on his usually transparent face.

"We gotta go!" Graham yelled, his voice awash in panic. In the distance he could see several men emerge from the train and start to run toward them.

Bedford pulled a handkerchief out of his pocket and reached down, picking something up and folding the cloth around it several times before putting it back into his pocket and running back to join Graham. Struggling to his feet, Graham once again put his arm around Bedford's shoulder and, together, they ran back toward the woods. Reaching the tree line once again, the boys peered back to see the men approaching the Mr. Ames' destroyed body before they turned, looking toward woods in which the boys now stood.

"Let's move before they come after us."

"What in the hell did you pick up back there, Bedford?"

He took the handkerchief from his pocket once more, opening it slowly. Graham looked on, at first confused about what the cloth held but, slowly and with a wave of disgust overtaking him, recognizing that it held the man's severed, bloody finger.

"Jesus, Bedford, why in God's name did you take that man's finger?"

"Souvenir," he replied evenly.

Nearly an hour later, Graham left Bedford at his house at the end of the block and headed home, his body still shaking with adrenaline. Nearing his yard, he saw Hattie walking toward the front door. "Hattie," he called out, beginning to run toward her. Her look of surprise was overtaken by concern as she saw the tears that streaked Graham's dusty cheeks. Wrapping his arms around her waist, he buried his head into her soft, round stomach and began to sob. She pulled him closer, voice warm. "What's done happened baby? What happened to you?" Kneeling down, she took his face in her hands and smiled reassuringly. "It's okay now, honey. Tell me what happened out there today."

FIFTEEN

"That," Dr. Clarice said seriously, "is a very disturbing image."

"Yes, I suppose it is. Actually, I would say that was the first time tension appeared in our friendship. It was a tension that grew over the next few years, before Bedford finally moved away." Graham recalled another incident, two summers later and only months before Bedford's mother announced that the family would relocate.

"Graham," Bedford had announced one morning, "I've got something to show you."

"What is it?" he asked, his curiosity piqued.

"I'll take you there."

The boys mounted their bicycles and rode across town, Bedford in the lead, until, at the end of a long paved road, they approached a wall of pine trees and a small gravel path leading into the thicket. "This way," Bedford urged, and the boys dropped their bikes and continued on by foot. After several moments, the pine trees began to thin, revealing a small cave in a wall of dirt and rock. In spite of his endless summertime explorations throughout their small town, this was a place that Graham had never seen before.

"Here we are," Bedford confirmed.

Someone had been in the cave before them, likely recently. Peering inside, Graham saw several half-smoked cigarettes and a number of candy bar wrappers from Now & Laters, Swedish Fish and Cadbury Creme Eggs, all Bedford's favorites, strewn across the dusty ground. Further on, he saw several stacks of magazines, their covers dirty and crumpled, colors faded with time.

"Whose stuff is this?" Graham asked, concerned that they'd be found intruding.

"Why, it's mine," Bedford replied.

Graham was surprised that his friend had kept such a place from him. How long had he been coming here? And given that the two spent almost ever summer day together, when would he have had the time? He felt uneasy, wondering what other secrets might be revealed.

"Have a look at these magazines I've been collecting," Bedford urged.

Graham entered the cave and looked down at a magazine, startled to find an image of a woman on the cover. She leaned forward, hands on her knees. Her naked breasts, wide and heavy, hung down from her chest, each terminating in a large, dark red nipple. Her eyes were opened wide and her face expressed an unfamiliar hunger.

"What in the world is this here, man?" he asked, unable to hide the alarm in his voice.

"Don't get your knickers in a knot," Bedford replied. "It's just some dirty magazines."

"Where in the hell did you get these?"

"I found 'em in the garage, in a box of stuff my paw left behind before he blew out of town. My mom put all that stuff in there so she wouldn't have to look at it, I guess."

Looking back down at the magazine, Graham felt a powerful urge to run, to leave the cave and to peddle his bicycle as quickly as possible home where, though he could not say why, he imagined that he would find relief. Did all men look at magazines like these? Did his father? His mother had said so often, her voice shot through with disgust and anxiety, that grown men were driven by an insatiable appetite. For most of his life, Graham had been confused. What was this appetite *for?* It was only recently that he had started to understand. It was for this, what he saw on the magazine cover before him.

His urge to know overcoming his terror of what he might find, he slowly picked up the top magazine in the first stack, opening it and feeling its weight in his hand. Taking a deep breath, he turned to a random page. An advertisement featured a solider holding a small, white square with a circular piece of plastic inside—in hindsight, he recognized the item to be a condom, but at the time he had no idea what this thing might be. To the left, in large black letters, were the words, "I take one everywhere I take my penis!" What in the world was the advertisement selling? Graham didn't know but it seemed strange to him.

"Look at this here," Bedford said, extending another magazine to him, already open. Graham saw a blond woman, her puffy, red lips curled upward in a smile. The woman was entirely naked. Feeling sick, Graham followed the trail of her body downward, past her generous breasts, one of which she seemed to be holding tightly, until he reached the space between her legs, which was covered in generous, black hair. He had never seen hair in that area before, save the few times his father had left his bedroom door open while changing into his evening clothes. Below the hair was an organ—he didn't know what else to call it—that was shaped like a pear, two large flaps of swollen flesh surrounding darker skin and, at the center, an even darker hole. It looked to him as if the woman had been stabbed and injured in a particularly grisly assault.

Dropping the magazine, Graham shrieked, "I don't want to see this, Bedford!"

"Stop pitchin' a hissy fit," Bedford replied angrily.

Graham ran to his bicycle, tears beginning to form, whether of anger or despair he could not be certain. How could this be what his friends were so excited about, so eager to experience? It seemed so violating to view a woman—especially a woman he didn't know and certainly didn't love—in such a pose. Reaching his bicycle, Graham pedaled back to town, leaving his friend in the cave.

The two boys didn't speak again for several weeks and, when they finally began, tentatively, to spend time together again, neither mentioned the incident. Graham never mentioned the incident to anyone else, either, although a few times he had considered speaking with his father.

Returning from his thoughts, Graham spoke. "I haven't seen Bedford in probably five years. He and his mother, Rosie, moved out of the area right after he turned 15. She met a man—an insurance salesman who had come through town selling, well, insurance—who lived in Memphis, the largest nearby city. After dating for a couple of months, she decided to relocate the family before the school year began. I didn't talk to Bedford very often after that—they had no reason to come back to where I lived and I certainly didn't have the means to get to Memphis—and about five years ago, we lost touch entirely. But up until they left, at least, he still had that finger in a sealed jar he kept in his bedside table, preserved in formaldehyde he stole from our science teacher." Concluding his story, he sighed.

Dr. Clarice's thoughts drifted toward a place that, gratefully, she was no longer forced to visit often, though the pain and despair of that time had turned to an ever-present sadness, a background accompaniment that shaped the texture of her life in almost every moment. Only two years after the birth of her daughter, she and her then-husband were delighted with the promise of a second child. Having proceeded through her first pregnancy and the birth of her daughter without complication, she had naturally assumed that the birth of her second child would follow suit. After all, medicine had, thankfully, progressed immensely over the past few generations and birth was no longer the fraught event that it had once been. And, in fact, the second birth was easier than her first, leaving her delighted, if exhausted, holding her newborn son at its conclusion.

Within a few moments, it became clear that something was wrong with the child. His skin began to turn blue and he struggled to breathe. Alerting the nurses immediately, they soon summoned a doctor. Clarice's son was pulled from her arms and rushed into surgery. Hours later, the same doctor returned and informed her, his voice without emotion, that her son had died. The boy was born without a pulmonary valve, which carries blood from the lower right chamber of the heart to the pulmonary artery, which in turn sends blood from the heart to the lungs. *Pulmonary atresia*, he called it in cold, medical language. By this time, Clarice's husband had been allowed into the room. Upon hearing the doctor's words, he immediately left the hospital to compose himself. That, she now realized, was the beginning of the rift between them, as she entered a deep grieving process...a process in which he could not join her.

The loss of her son, she now felt, could only be described with one word—horror. Horror, after all, was the bursting forth of the unthinkable into a world that had previously seemed comprehensible, even if variously painful and disappointing. Her son's death had defied all of what she had taken for granted: that he would grow into adulthood and continue living after she herself had died. With his death, she had been forced to confront the emotional reality of an indisputable truth, that the world does not exist for us and, at any moment, can defy our consoling fantasies of order and control. Over the coming year, the tendrils of that horror reached into each area of her life and wrought destruction. Her marriage crumbled under the strain of the loss as well as the financial security she had taken for granted. The newfound necessity of supporting herself, in addition to the demand that she make meaning of this loss and upheaval, led her to pursue a career as a psychologist and, after her daughter left for college, as a psychoanalyst.

Dr. Clarice reflected on her reverie. Why was she thinking about all of this now? These losses and the meaning that she had made of them had certainly been a central theme in her personal psychoanalysis, entailing an extended process of grief. But her analysis had concluded many years ago and these losses had been largely laid to rest, revisiting only briefly from time to time as she grew older. What was it, she asked herself, that brought them to mind once again? Perhaps it was the emergence of Mr. Ames in Graham's story, a hatchet-wielding madman intent on murder suddenly appearing to two boys out in the woods on a summer afternoon. That, without a doubt, could be described as a horrific incident. Yet she felt that this didn't entirely capture her reaction. There was a foreboding in the room, as if some further horror would soon emerge in her patient's story, something even more disturbing that Mr. Ames.

SIXTEEN

"**S**weetheart," Hattie said, stroking his hair, "let's take a walk before dinnertime. You tell me what's done happened to you today, you hear?" With that, she began to walk down the driveway, Graham quickly falling in beside her. Her shoes, a pair of black flats received as a Christmas gift from Henry and now worn with age, squeaked with each step. Her movement was slow and steady, though Graham had occasionally heard her refer to her "arthritis" when speaking with his father, which he knew caused her some sort of pain.

"So what got you so upset, honey?" she asked.

"You wouldn't believe me if I told you."

"Try me," she replied, her voice firm with certainty.

He began to speak, the story tumbling out with a desperation that surprised him. He had not anticipated that describing the afternoon's events would bring such relief, and he was grateful that she listened without judgment or critique. He knew, too, that she would never relay the story to his mother or father. As he talked, the tension in his belly began to ease and, with each affirming hum he received in response, his guilt faded away slightly. He concluded by telling her that Bedford had taken a "souvenir"—the man's finger, wrapping it in a white handkerchief and putting it into his pocket—from the scene of the accident. What Bedford's intention was for the finger, Graham didn't know.

"Oh Lord," Hattie remarked upon hearing about the finger, "I always did get the feelin' there might be somethin' amiss about that boy, what with the stories 'bout his father and all. You'll need to be watchin' yourself around him, hear?"

He nodded. Although in the past he would have dismissed such a suggestion without much thought—Bedford was his best friend, after all—the boy's decision to keep Mr. Ames' finger disturbed him. The man, though clearly deranged, had still been a human being, feelings and all, and it was disrespectful to treat his body as a mere token.

Without realizing it, the pair had reached the end of the street where there were several lots without houses, the empty land covered in tall weeds and an assortment of magnolia and pine trees. He sighed with relief, for the story had been told and he was exhausted from the telling.

"Hey, Graham!"

He glanced back and forth, failing to find the source of the voice.

"Up here!" the voice came again, excited.

His eyes followed the trunk of a large magnolia tree, searching for a face amidst the tangle of branches and leaves. Near the top he saw Dan, a freckle-faced boy several years older than Graham who attended his school. Dan looked down at him, laughing. He was an impish, arrogant child who often fought with his classmates, losing each time, and he enjoyed bullying the younger school children, bragging about his dominations over lunch in the cafeteria. Graham's mother, in that conspiratorial tone reserved only for gossip, said that Dan's father had abandoned the family after falling in love with the music director at the Methodist church, leaving them both covered in sin. Although Graham didn't like Dan, particularly because of how he treated the younger kids, he felt sorry for him.

"Who's that you're with?" Dan asked.

"That's Hattie," he replied. "She's our family's housekeeper."

"Oh, that right?" Dan called out, his voice mocking this time. "What're you doin' with her, then? Walkin' down the street with your black maid?"

Graham's face grew hot, a flush of anger making its way through his veins. "Don't you say that!" he said coldly. "You're not gonna speak 'bout Hattie like that around here."

"Why not? She's just a nigger," Dan replied, his voice taunting and his smile wide.

Hattie put her hand on Graham's shoulder. "Don't you worry yourself over it, honey," she reassured him. He looked up, meeting her brown eyes, in which he could see the barely concealed hurt Dan's words had caused. Alongside the hurt, though, there was something else that he had never seen before. Weariness and resignation, perhaps?

Graham slowly walked over to the magnolia tree and began to climb, first wrapping his legs around the trunk and then, grabbing a low branch to maintain his position, lifting a leg up and over a higher branch. Having spent many summer afternoons climbing trees with Bedford, he was a confident and quick. He had learned to ignore the burn of the tree's bark on his hands and to use his legs as a source of strength, relying on his arms only to steady himself as he rapidly made his way to the top. Reaching Dan, whose laughter now had an edge of uncertainty, he grabbed the collar of the boy's shirt, stained yellow with dirt and sweat, and pulled him close enough that he could smell the stink of his breath, hot against his face, and see the dusty grime that covered the boy's forehead and neck.

"Don't you ever say that again, you hear?" His voice was a low growl, utterly unfamiliar to him. "You have no right to speak like that." He was surprised that events were unfolding as they were. Though aware of the rage that filled him, he felt, somehow, that he was watching himself from the outside, that his rage was not his own.

Without warning, Graham pulled harder, bringing the boy to the edge of the branch. Dan's eyes opened wide with fear as he realized he might fall. His mouth opened in angry protest but, before he could speak, Graham tugged, hard, a final time. Dan's arms flailed, making large windmills in a futile attempt to regain his balance before, finally, he lost his grip on the branch and began to fall. Even as Dan fell, Graham wondered why he had decided to pull that final time, what force inside him had acted, almost without his consent, to propel all three of them onto a path with an uncertain fate. For what felt like several moments there was no sound, for Dan was entirely quiet as he fell until he hit the ground with a large thump. Hattie gasped, hands to her mouth, and Graham began the careful climb down, a pit of dread taking up residence in his gut.

"Oh, Jesus," Hattie said quietly, "Jesus help me."

With Graham on the ground beside Hattie once more, the two stared at Dan silently. When the boy finally he stirred, first groaning quietly and then cradling his left arm, apparently hurt, Hattie sighed in relief. Several moments passed with the pair still looking on, frozen, each dreading what the future might bring. Finally the boy sat up and opened his eyes, still holding his arm, and began to wail, spit flying from his mouth as his face reddened, tears quickly wetting his cheeks.

"Oh, Jesus," Hattie said again, relief in her voice this time.

She rushed over and kneeled next to Dan. "Boy, let me see your arm." His defiance gone, he held it out as she ran her hands over it, bending it slightly. "I don't think it's broke," she said, finally, "and thank the good Lord for that." Receiving no reply but only a blank stare, she continued. "You run on home to your mama and ask her for a pack of ice, you hear? That's sure to help the healin'." Dan scrambled to his feet, still shedding silent tears, a look of confused shock on his dust-streaked face, and ran down the road toward his family's home without a further word.

"Lord help us, Graham," Hattie said softly, "that boy's mama gonna cause a world of trouble for both of us, believe me. We best get back home now."

A short time later, he followed Hattie into the front door where they found Dottie sitting at the kitchen table, a newspaper that was several days old in her hands and a half-full cup of coffee on the table beside her. Graham wondered whether it was the same cup she'd had earlier in the day, now cold and stale. His mother tended to carry around the same cup of coffee throughout the day, never finishing it.

"Graham, I've been praying' myself to death about you all day," she said, her voice anxious with concern. "I was just sittin' here thinking you might've gotten hurt down at that roller rink. Thank the good Lord you're home safe."

"It's okay, Mom," he reassured her, still preoccupied with the events that had transpired only minutes before. "It's really not that dangerous."

"Oh, dear," Dottie said, seeming not to hear her son's response but clearly wearied by her waiting. "The other thing preying on my mind, son," she continued, her voice now a conspiratorial whisper, "is what you done found down at the shoe store. Was your father up to any mischief? Tell me that, will you?"

He had been expecting his mother's question, for she asked him each time he returned from his father's store. This time, however, he was uncertain how to respond. He *had* seen something at the store that had troubled him deeply: his father talked with Mrs. Jones in a way that he had never heard him talk with another woman before, not even his own wife…suggesting he had an interest in her that was more than merely professional. At the same time, Graham didn't want to bring trouble to his father, who was always kind to him. He felt, in a way that he could not express in words, that if his relationship with his father was threatened, then his own well-being, even his life itself, might be imperiled. His innards clenched with worry.

"Mom, I didn't see anything to worry about. Dad was just selling shoes."

"I see. Thanks for lettin' me know, son. Now, I've just worn myself out with all this worry. I'm goin' to put on my dressing gown and get to sleep for the evenin'. It's been just a terrible day, you see? Well, Hattie, be so kind as to look after the boy's supper, would you? Henry's too, if you don't mind."

With that, Dottie stood and left the kitchen, making her way to the back of the house with the seeming intent to sleep, though it was still early in the evening. Hattie and Graham looked at each other, fear animating both their faces, for several moments in silence. Before either could speak, the silence was broken by the sound of the phone ringing.

SEVENTEEN

Dr. Clarice tried to turn her attention back to Graham's story, but in the corners of her mind she continued to reflect on the child she had lost so long ago. Against the doctor's advice, she had demanded to see her son's body. Even now, she remembered the cold, white walls of the hospital morgue and the hard, metal rolling table that child had been laid upon. Though his little chest had been sewn up in the most cursory fashion, a poor attempt to hide the violence to his small body in an effort to save his life, he nonetheless seemed so still, so peaceful. She would never forget bending down to kiss his pale, blue hand. In hindsight, she understood the doctor's advice—these images would accompany her for the remainder of her days on earth—yet she did not regret that she had insisted on seeing her child one last time.

She had also insisted he be buried, with a gravestone of his own, in the midst of the cemetery, surrounding by green grass. Though he disagreed with her decision, preferring that the child be cremated and then forgotten, her husband had been tolerant of it at first. As the months passed and she visited the grave each week, leaving flowers behind every time, his tolerance slowly turned to anger and, finally, to contempt. Yes, she had grieved intensely for several years; and though she had hidden most of her grief from her daughter, it had infiltrated her relationship with her husband. He had been largely unable to grieve, never visiting his son's grave. Instead, his sadness and anger congealed into a hard mass that covered his heart, pulling him away from her and his family to spend more time at the office. That she had not been able to keep the marriage alive for her daughter's sake was one of her deepest regrets. Now, she willed herself to set these thoughts aside once more, this time more forcefully and with a promise to herself that she would return to them later, when she was unoccupied.

"That's a powerful story. There's a lot there, isn't there?" she commented. "Something you had been storing up inside—powerful aggression—seems to have burst out without warning. You also said that you felt detached—like watching yourself from the outside—as all this happened."

Dr. Clarice picked up the coffee cup from the table beside her chair, lifting it to her mouth to drink. Graham wondered whether she might cut her mouth on the cup's cracked lip. As she took a quick drink, her rings clinked against the cup's ceramic surface. She wore two rings on her left hand, one on her ring finger and another on her index finger. The former, as best he could tell, was made of a golden metal, a green stone in its setting. He couldn't discern whether this was a wedding ring and, given the intensity of the interaction when he'd asked her where she grew up, decided not to inquire. Even from across the room, he could hear the sound of her swallowing the cup's dark, milky liquid.

"Yes, that's the best way that I can describe it. I still remember this like it was yesterday." He paused, gathering his thoughts. "I've always had a problematic relationship to aggression. I've never really spoken to anyone about this before, but I suppose if there's ever a place to talk about it, it's here, isn't it?"

"That's what we're here for," she affirmed.

In the fifth grade, Graham and Bedford had been almost inseparable. The pair had become friends several years ago when Graham discovered his neighbor in the woods near his home. Bedford, it turned out, lived at the end of the block with his mother, Mrs. Rosie, who worked in the building that housed his father's shoe store. Both boys had been searching for a way to occupy their long summer afternoons and that very day set to building a fort out of broken branches and logs cut, only with great effort and persistence, with Graham's hatchet. At the day's end, both boys were covered in sweat and dust and for the first time in weeks, felt relief from the gnawing loneliness of the summer's isolation.

When they first met, Bedford had been a year ahead of Graham in school but due to poor marks that year—which Dottie frequently mentioned were due to "home troubles," a phrase she uttered like a curse and with a disdainful frown—had been required to repeat the grade. Almost immediately after their friendship began, the boys began to have classes together. Graham's teachers often commented that Bedford distracted him from "realizing his potential," a thought that worried him in his more reflective moments.

To their teacher's dismay, the boys spent many hours in school inventing games to pass the time. Bedford introduced Graham to the game of "pencil break," which required one boy to hold a pencil horizontally, one hand gripping the eraser and the other the lead. The opponent would then flick his pencil downward, as quickly as possible, in an effort to break the horizontal pencil. They would take turns until one of the pencils inevitably shattered. Graham could remember, even now, the scorn that Mrs. Needle, their teacher, heaped upon them when she found the boys playing the game instead of working on problem sets or writing assignments. "You foolish boys," she hissed, "are wastin' good pencils."

One afternoon, when only one pencil remained unbroken, Graham introduced a new game of his own invention. It required, he explained, that one boy lay his hand flat, palm down, upon the writing desk. The other boy would hold the remaining pencil at shoulder height until the first gave a nod. At that point, he would try to stab his opponent's flat hand before he could pull it away. They would take turns stabbing until one managed to strike his target.

Because the game was his invention, Graham would strike first. Feeling little concern and ignoring the anxiety coloring Bedford's face, he held his pencil at shoulder height and waited. Reluctantly, Bedford placed his hand upon the writing desk and nodded. Graham stabbed, surprised when the pencil impacted the top of his friend's hand, piercing the flap of skin between his index and middle fingers. Bedford howled in pain as blood began to leak onto the table, the pencil remaining firmly lodged in his skin. As he recognized what he had done, Graham's eyes widened with fear.

"What in Jesus' name has happened here, boy?" Mrs. Needle stared down at him, hands on her hips and her mouth drawn into a tight line. "You two boys are always acting like heathens from the backwoods, but now you've gone and done it, Graham. You've hurt Bedford real bad."

Graham looked up at her, smiling with embarrassment.

"You think this is a joke, boy?" she demanded.

"No, ma'am, I didn't mean to hurt Bedford."

"Explain to me, Graham, how in the world you thought stabbing that pencil into his hand wouldn't hurt him, would you please?"

Graham's face flushed with guilt as his body vibrated with adrenaline. He felt cornered, unable to escape the woman's wrath.

She looked down at him, her gray hair pulled into a tight bun and the bones of her thin face accentuated even further as her jaw muscles flexed with anger. He wanted more than anything to run, to hide in the hallway or, even better, in his room at home, upstairs, with the door shut tightly behind him. Receiving only Graham's silence in response, Mrs. Needle reached down and grabbed his arm, her bony hand gripping him tightly and pulling him toward her. She pulled a foot-long wooden ruler from a pocket in her blouse and lifted it high. "This," she said, her eyes wild with rage, "is what you get for behaving badly. I won't be sparin' you any more."

With that, she brought the ruler down, hard, on his knuckles. Gasping with pain, he tried to pull his arm away but she held tight and brought the ruler down a second, and then a third, time.

"Let me go, bitch!" Graham cried desperately.

"What did you say, boy? What was that?" she shrieked, her cheeks red.

"I didn't say nothin', ma'am," he said, recovering his composure.

"Don't piss on my leg, boy! I heard what you said. How dare you? I'll see you to the principal's office myself." She pulled Graham to his feet, turning over his writing desk in the process, and marched toward the door as he stumbled along beside her, still trying to free his arm. As the door slammed behind them, Bedford sat in his chair, stunned, and continued to bleed freely.

"What do you think," Dr. Clarice now queried, "led you to invent such a dangerous game?"

"I've never understood it myself," Graham replied, "because it's obvious that someone was going to get hurt and I never had any conscious intent to hurt Bedford. He was a really good friend to me for the most part, at least until our relationship went sour. Looking back, it seems like I was 'going through the motions'—inventing and playing an especially aggressive game—without even thinking about what I was doing."

"Without thinking about what you were doing." she said thoughtfully, "you were able to express your aggression without having to take conscious responsibility for it as your own. From what you've told me about your family, it wouldn't have been safe to express aggression, even in appropriate ways, in the home."

"Yes," he nodded, "that certainly seems true. I don't know what my mother, in particular, would have done if I'd gotten angry. Though I had reason to."

"Perhaps you felt that you could lose the tenuous attachment you had with her."

He nodded. "That makes sense. You know, there's more to this story. I'm not sure it relates to what we're talking about at the moment, but to get it off my chest, let me go ahead and tell you what happened next. I know we don't have much time left, so I'll tell you quickly and then we can get back to what happened on the day in my life that I've been describing for most of our session today."

"Yes," Dr. Clarice said evenly.

"So Mrs. Needle took me to the principal's office and left me there, telling the secretary what had happened. When the principal— he was a tall, black-haired man who had a doctorate, which I think was probably unusual, especially in those days, for a principal—came out, the secretary relayed the story. The main thing she emphasized—I don't know why she did this—was that I'd called Mrs. Needle a bitch."

He paused, his face reddening. "This is embarrassing. When I was talking with the principal, I insisted that the teacher had a grudge against me and had fabricated her complaint. I don't remember much about the conversation, but somehow I convinced him that I was telling the truth. He didn't punish me at all. Can you believe that?"

"Yes," she nodded, "I suppose that I can. You were a precocious child, it seems, and probably verbally deft enough to be convincing."

Graham paused, thinking about an incident that occurred many years later. On a visit home from college for a week to see his father, he had taken the green Oldsmobile, now barely serviceable, to the town's video rental store. As he searched for a film with which to occupy himself for the evening, he heard a strident hiss. Looking up, he saw an old woman, her white hair pulled into a tight bun and her face drawn with age, staring at him.

"Don't you remember me, boy?" she asked.

When he didn't reply, she continued. "It's me, Mrs. Needle!"

His eyes widened.

"Yes," she spat, "You remember me, boy. Well, what a terrible time I had because of you. You're a damn liar, you know that? After you told that principal those lies, it never was the same for me. But you'll get yours. Jesus is gonna cut your tail, you hear?"

Terrified by the woman's ire and disturbed by his own guilt, he dropped the cassette he had chosen back on the shelf, and, without reply, walked quickly from the store. Back in his father's car, he took several deep breaths before he turned the key—three attempts were required before the engine roared to life—and drove home.

"I feel terrible, because she must have been reprimanded by the principal. That has to be the most ruthless thing that I have ever done to another person."

"There's a lot to say about this. One thing we're seeing," Dr. Clarice suggested, "is that you have a complicated relationship with your aggression. As we discussed earlier, at times it's inhibited, even profoundly so as in your sexual encounters. At other times, it seems to burst forth, uncontrolled, and does damage to the people around you. And that makes sense, doesn't it? You have every reason to be tremendously angry about what you've gone through. But knowing at some level that you carry so much anger, you're inclined to keep it under wraps because you've seen how much damage is done when it gets out."

"Yes. I know we're almost out of time," he replied, turning to look at the digital clock behind him. "Wow, there's only about five minutes left, right? We have fifty minutes total?" She nodded and he continued. "Let me finish up the story about the day I've been describing and we can come back to some of this when we meet again."

EIGHTEEN

Hattie and Graham continued to stare at each other, the phone's loud ring punctuating the silence at regular intervals. After the fifth ring, she exhaled. "Help me, Jesus," she muttered as she went to the phone and lifted the receiver to her ear. Even from where he now sat, uncertain that he could maintain his balance if he remained standing, Graham could hear the voice on the other end of the line.

"This here is Gertrude Smith. Dan's mother. I'm callin' because my son just came home brutalized, says that your son pushed him out of a tree. Now he's hurt his arm, and maybe other parts besides, and he tells me that your black maid just looked on."

"I'm sorry, ma'am," she said softly, "I'm Hattie, the family's maid. Henry and Dottie aren't available right now, but I can have them call you back."

"Sweet Jesus," the voice on the phone grew louder, "you're the one! You was there and you didn't raise a hand to protect my boy from gettin' pushed out that tree!"

"Ma'am, the boys had an accident, that's for sure. But you know that boys play rough sometimes, and I don't think neither of them meant the other harm. If there's anybody at fault, it's me for lettin' them in that tree. I made sure that your boy's arm weren't broke and then I sent him straight home to find you."

"Well," she replied, "that ain't enough for me, you hear? I'm gonna talk to Henry myself. I know him from down at the shoe store, where I shop myself. You're fixin' to be out of a job, you hear? That's what I'm gonna do, yes I am."

"Ma'am," Hattie said slowly, "I thinkin' we might—"

The phone clicked and went silent for several moments until a dial tone sounded.

"Well," she sighed, and put the receiver back in its cradle, "she was madder than a wet hen. There just weren't no talkin' reason to her, none at all."

"Hattie," Graham replied, "I'm gonna talk to my father and tell him it was all my fault, that you didn't have nothin' to do with any of this."

"No," she replied firmly, "that's not somethin' you're gonna do. I'm grown and you ain't and I mean to take responsibility, even if it leaves me out of a job." She turned and walked out of the kitchen and into the laundry room. Her chest was tight, for she didn't know how Henry would react to Mrs. Smith's anger. She knew him to be a reasonable man—he had shown her his generosity and kindness on many occasions—but she also knew that he was susceptible to influence from his wife. Yes, if Dottie got wind of this, she'd likely insist that Hattie be turned out of their home that same day, never to return. Well, what could she do? She'd have to turn this matter over to the Lord, for control was not in her hands.

Now, Hattie turned her mind to the tasks that remained for the day. Pulling out a clean white blouse from the blue plastic basket beside the washing machine and dryer, she laid the garment out on the long, white ironing board. She plugged in the iron and waited until the surface was hot. Pressing a button on the iron's nose, steam rose up, covering her face in wet mist. As she worked, she thanked the Lord that the electric iron had been invented only a few years ago. In times past, the process had been more arduous, requiring that she place a flatiron directly on a fire or atop the stove, re-warming it often. With a smile of gratitude, she picked up the iron by its handle and drew it across the fabric, spraying starch as she went.

In this way, nearly an hour passed as Hattie worked through an assortment of blouses, slacks and shirts. As she neared the end of her task, Graham walked into the laundry room, a worried look on his face, and climbed atop the washing machine, where he often sat while Hattie tended to the ironing. At times, with her close supervision, she would allow him to iron a piece or two. He delighted in spraying the starch and ejecting the steam, which reminded Hattie that children often found joy in those tasks that had become mundane and routine for the grown. She knew that he was troubled.

"What's on your mind, dear?"

"I'm still thinkin' about what happened this afternoon and what's comin'."

"Oh, sweetheart," she replied in a soothing tone, "Don't you worry. I'm gonna talk to your father. He's a clear-headed and good man, that's for sure, and I think he'll understand the situation just right. And we'll do our best to keep wind of all that's happened from gettin' to your mother, you hear?"

"Yes, but—"

"Honey, you just have to hand it over to the Lord. There's nothin' we can do."

"Hattie, I'm sorry."

"Oh, dear," she said, turning to face him directly. "You got nothin' to be sorry for. Nothin' at all. You've got yourself a good and kind heart, you hear me? Don't neglect it."

He knew that the discussion had been laid to rest. Several moments passed between them in silence as she finished pressing the last garment and, turning off and unplugging the iron, hung the shirt on a wire hanger next to all the others. Brushing her hands together with a satisfied smile, she went into the kitchen, busying herself with pots and pans, several containing food that she had prepared earlier in the day to be stored in the refrigerator. "Graham, sweetie," she called from the kitchen, "you go on and get washed up. I'll have supper ready in about an hour."

As he washed his hands and face, Graham worried about the events that had unfolded at the road's end. What had come over him, that he had attacked another boy, throwing him from a tree? He could have killed him. "You have to be careful in this world, son," Dottie often reminded him, "for only a single misstep can ruin the rest of your life. Your father and I won't be able to help you." He passed the next hour with thoughts like these as he sat at the dining table, waiting for his father to return from work.

Soon his father came home. Smiling at his son, Henry set his briefcase by the front door and took a seat across from Graham at the table. Graham excused himself to help Hattie in the kitchen. He breathed in the familiar warm smell of food cooking as Hattie stirred a large pot.

"Hattie," he asked quietly, unable to lay the matter to rest. "Do you think Dan's mama is gonna talk to my parents?"

"I don't know, honey," she replied evenly, "but it's best to let the Lord take care of it. What can we do now, anyhow? What's done is done. I'll talk to your father."

Hattie's calm words took the edge off the dread filling Graham's chest. Without further comment on the matter, she handed him a large bowl of black-eyed peas. "Set that on the table in there, would you dear?" Moments later, she followed him to the table with a basket full of cornbread, smothered in melting butter, and a plate covered in fried chicken, grease beginning to pool beneath the crispy brown thighs and drumsticks.

"This looks lovely, Hattie," Henry said, looking up from his newspaper. "I appreciate you stayin' here late this evening, what with Dottie having taken to the bed early"

"Yes sir," she replied, "it's no trouble. She seemed to be afflicted this evenin', I am sorry to say." Henry grunted, biting into a piece of cornbread before licking his greasy lips.

"I've got to tell you, sir, 'bout what happened this afternoon, "Hattie said carefully. "Graham and I was out walkin' and we came across this other boy down at the end of the road—"

"Yes, Hattie," Henry said. "That boy's mother, Gertrude, stopped by the store this afternoon, mad as a hornet! She told me that Graham here pushed her son out of a tree and that you stood by while it happened. Now, I know that my son ain't inclined to violence and I know that you're a good, God-fearing woman, and that's what I told her. I'm thinkin' that all of what happened must've been an accident, ain't that right?"

"Yes sir," she nodded, "Graham didn't mean no harm and I tended to the boy as best I could. But if anybody's at fault, it's me, that's for sure."

"No, Hattie, you may be grown but you can't stop every mishap. When I was a boy, I got hurt often enough runnin' around in these here woods. Let's not worry over it."

"Thank you, sir," she replied, relief washing over her face. "Well, if that's all you need for the day, then I best be on my way home to my husband."

"One more thing, Hattie," Henry said. Hattie, halfway to the kitchen, turned around to face Henry. "Let's make sure not to mention this to the missus. No need to worry her."

"Yes, sir."

A few moments later, Hattie emerged from the kitchen wearing a long khaki overcoat and carrying a brown leather purse and a large cloth bag. As she approached the door she turned back to the dining table, seemingly hesitant to speak.

"Graham, dear," she said, taking a wrapped box from her bag, "this here is a present for your birthday. I hope you enjoy it." Graham took the gift from her, smiling broadly with surprise. He had forgotten it was his birthday, then remembered the date circled on the calendar on his bulletin board upstairs. Today, he thought without any particular emotion, he was eight years old. By the time he had recovered from his thoughts, Hattie had walked out the front door, closing it softly behind her.

Henry, a cloud of guilt forming around his heart, realized with alarm that he had forgotten his son's birthday. His mind had been so occupied with that damn Mrs. Jones, that he had failed to look after his own son. He had been lusting after a woman—a married woman, at that!—all the while forgetting the one day each year a father should never overlook. Perhaps his wife was right: he was a depraved animal, slave to his base instincts. Yes, perhaps she knew him better than he knew himself.

Graham looked up to see his father staring at him, his face a mixture of worry and regret. After what he'd seen earlier in the day at the shoe store, he was frightened by the complex mixture of feelings that stirred inside him. He didn't know whether to be angry or sad, disappointed or confused. He placed Hattie's gift in the chair next to him and picked up a piece of chicken, blowing on it for several moments before taking a bite. It was crispy, slightly burned, and its oily coating still sizzled. It burned his tongue.

NINETEEN

"That speaks to a tremendous strength of character, doesn't it?" Dr. Clarice asked, rhetorically. "Hattie was willing to take responsibility for the incident entirely, even though she had so much to lose, to protect you and because she recognized she was the adult."

She admired this woman, Hattie, who had clearly been so helpful to her patient throughout his development. As his story unfolded, she was struck, again and again, by Hattie's kindness to him. That relationship must account, at least in part, for many of the strengths she observed in him. She had been surprised that he had managed to speak so directly about such troubling topics in their first session. He had even talked about his sexuality twice: notable, given the intensity of the anxiety and shame he associated with it. Many patients, even those far less inhibited than he, needed their relationship with her to deepen before they felt comfortable speaking openly about this area of their lives which, while absolutely important, was also the nexus of so much guilt, shame and confusion. It suggested a hopeful prognosis, she thought, that Graham had the ego strength to persist in putting his feelings into words, in spite of the difficult emotions that he continued to struggle with. She looked forward to working with this young man.

"Yes, she really did. It's painful that both Hattie and George—people whom society, at least then and there, regarded as different, lesser—showed far more character than my own parents. I was very lucky to have had them in my life."

"Your father's response is interesting," mused Dr. Clarice. "He behaved quite generously toward both of you. At the same time, his response strikes me as somewhat indifferent. Most parents would have done more investigating to find out what really happened between you and Dan and what Hattie's role was in all of it. Perhaps he should have been more concerned."

"I've never thought of that," he replied. "I can see what you're saying. He didn't seem in the least bit worried. That's surprising, because he usually got quite distraught when someone in the community was upset with him, on account of his shoe store and wanting to have a good name so that people would shop there. Or so he said."

"I'm wondering whether he was, in fact, involved with that woman you mentioned."

"Mrs. Jones," Graham affirmed. "Yes, I don't know, even to this day, what to think about that. Since my mother died, as far as I know at least, my father has never dated again. He certainly hasn't remarried. It seems to me that if he were the type to have an affair, he would've remarried, or at least dated, by now."

"Yes, it's curious," she agreed.

The two sat in silence for several moments, both aware that this was a question that, at least for now, they could not answer. Graham could hear the clock ticking softly behind him. Outside, the rain continued to fall, lighter now. He wondered whether, someday, he might ask his father if he had ever had an affair. He was sure the question would shock Henry, perhaps even offend him. He knew that many of the fathers in the community, at least according to his mother, had cheated on their wives. Bedford's father had in fact run off with another woman. Could he blame his own father if he had sought companionship outside of a marriage that must have been so depriving?

Graham now thought about the last time he had seen his friend Bedford, five years earlier. Though Bedford had moved to Memphis when the boys were still young, they had kept in touch by letter and had seen each other every couple of years when Graham's father had driven him to Memphis or, less often, when Bedford visited the small town with his mother. While Graham had attended a local state college, his friend had gone straight to work after high school, living with a group of young men in an overcrowded apartment in the capital, Jackson, and spending his days doing odd jobs. The summer after his first year of college, Graham visited Bedford in Jackson. He was shocked at the living conditions: there were half-melted candles on the floor throughout the apartment and dishes in the sink that had begun to mold. Bedford's friends spent most weeknights lying on the couch smoking marijuana—a substance Graham had never tried—and listening to music. On the weekends, they experimented with even more powerful substances.

In the evenings, Graham slept on that couch in the living room, yellowed and dusty and emitting a strong odor of mildew, surrounding by candles that were beginning to fade. One of Bedford's roommates owned a pet wolverine, the first one Graham had ever seen. The stocky, muscular creature was about the size of an average dog, but its claws were long and sharp. As Graham slept alone, in the dark, the animal often approached the couch and made a low, threatening noise, a cross between a growl and a snarl, staring at Graham with its small, unblinking eyes.

On the final night of his stay, a Friday, Bedford insisted that Graham accompany him to a party. They took the bus across town and walked up to a large, immaculate house with a heavy wooden door. Bedford knocked, hard, several times, until the door swung open and a beautiful young blonde woman looked out, blinking.

"Bedford, that you?" she asked, her voice hazy.

"Yes, Celeste," he replied, annoyance in his voice. "Let us in."

The living room was crowded with people. Several sat in corners, some alone and others in pairs. Some couples were engaged in varied erotic activities, seemingly oblivious to the other people in the room. One young man, thin and shirtless, sat in front of the wall, rubbing his hands up and down the wallpaper and moaning. As Graham looked on, the man seemed to become increasingly upset before, falling onto his back, he thrust his legs up the wall and began to shriek loudly. "Get them off me," he screamed again and again. Another man kneeled down next to him, speaking so softly that Graham couldn't hear, though his words seemed to offer the distressed man some comfort.

"Let's go back to the pool," Bedford urged, still sounding irritated.

Eager to leave the room as quickly as possible, Graham followed his friend. Before they reached the pool, Bedford stopped in front of a bathroom, its door open and revealing two young men inside who were looking down at a small pile of white powder. "Hey, Mac," Bedford said. "Let me get in on that." Pushing the two men aside, he picked up a small, thin straw and snorted powder into each nostril, coughing vigorously afterward. He gestured with the straw for Graham to take a turn with the drug.

"No, thanks," Graham said.

"You've gotta give this a shot, man."

"No, I don't."

"Suit yourself." The irritation in Bedford's voice grew. He walked past Graham and out into the back yard. There were people standing around the swimming pool, drinks in hand, and many more swimming in the pool itself. Very few, Graham noticed, had on swimsuits. Over the next hour, Bedford talked to a number of people, seeming to know each of them, as Graham followed along behind him. Graham was surprised to see how many drinks Bedford took: beer, wine, and even vodka.

As time passed, Bedford became increasingly agitated. Finally, he walked up to the diving board, pulling off his shirt, revealing a prodigious amount of chest hair.

"Here we go!" he yelled, the crowd going silent and turning their attention toward him. Bedford drew a lighter out of his pants pocket and, bringing it up to his chest, flicked the flint wheel once and, then, a second time. Suddenly, his chest hair burst into flame and, screaming incoherently, he jumped into the pool with a splash. People all around cheered.

Disgusted, Graham went back into the house and through the living room. He stepped over several youth who lay sprawled across the floor in various degrees of incoherence, and out onto the street. After 15 minutes of walking in the nighttime heat, he caught a taxi back to Bedford's apartment, where his own car was parked. Unable to get into the apartment to retrieve his clothes, he got into his car and began the long drive back to his father's house, where he spent the remainder of the summer before returning to school in the Fall.

Returning from his reverie, Graham wondered why he was thinking about his friend now. He had, after all, been thinking about his father and whether he had been involved with women outside of his marriage. Well, maybe it was better to leave some questions unasked. On the other hand, he felt he needed to understand more about why his childhood had been the way it was and who both of his parents were. He decided to wait and see what he might uncover in his work with Dr. Clarice before asking his father.

"As we're talking about your father," Dr. Clarice remarked, "I find myself wondering what you know about how he met your mother, how he decided to marry her. It seems to me she must have been quite ill even before they were married."

"I don't know much about that," Graham replied, a pensive look on his face, "but I can tell you what little I do know. My father's father ran a small grocery store out in the country. His mother, apparently, didn't work: she was in charge of the children full-time. From what my father says, he had a happy childhood and he tells a lot of suspenseful stories of adventure from his youth. As he describes it, he was quite the sportsman. He played both basketball and baseball well and was admired by all of his friends, especially the young women. My mother grew up in a small farmhouse. Her father was a cruel man. I only have a few memories of him, because he died when I was young, but I can recall him speaking with the most gruff, intimidating voice I've ever heard. My mother often made reference to him whipping her with a belt and threatening to turn her out of the house. I wonder if she was looking for a husband so that she could get away from her father. I gather that they met socially when my mother was visiting her aunt in the town where I grew up."

"We'll want to keep thinking about this more over time," Dr. Clarice said, "but from what you're saying, your mother was eager to escape an abusive father, to find someone to take care of her perhaps. I wonder whether she was resentful that your father wasn't able to take care of her as fully as she wished. He wasn't able to save her from her emotional pain."

"She was certainly resentful, that much is for sure." He paused, looking down at his hands, which were folded neatly in his lap. "Well," he sighed, "let me tell you the last part of the story. I know we're almost out of time. Probably this part deserves more attention that we're able to give it today, but that's okay. We can pick it up later."

TWENTY

Dottie awoke, her body slick with stale sweat, her eyes darting back and forth. She strained to make out the details of her surroundings, the shadows illuminated only by a dim shaft of light that issued from her bedroom door's improper alignment with its frame. Ever since she'd moved into this home, only a few months after she'd married Henry, the light had fractured the room's darkness, often keeping her from sleep and becoming an object of her frustrated ruminations. Henry had tried to right the door several times at her insistence, but it always returned in time to its original position, the rusty hinges unable to support its weight. But now, she was grateful for the light, for it allowed her to see that she was alone in the room, safe beneath her heavy quilt.

She'd been jolted awake by the same nightmare she'd been having for the past 25 years. The dream, she knew, was an exact replication of that terrible day in her childhood when her world was fractured, never to be whole again. It always began with her walking outside late in the evening, across the dusty expanse of lawn to her family's barn. When the screaming began between her parents—as it did on most evenings around this time—when her father was thoroughly inebriated on homemade moonshine, the barn was her refuge. This place had been more sacred than the long, hard pews of the church where she spent several evenings each week, plus the bulk of her weekends. She loved the company of the animals and the warm, moist smell of wet earth beneath her feet.

In the nightmare, as she had often done in real life, she pulled out a sack of marbles and drew a large circle on the dusty floor of the barn. Within moments she was absorbed in her game, as she pushed the shooter marble across the floor time and time again. As a child, it was in these moments that she forgot the constant tension that was her ongoing companion, that pit of dread taking up residence in her stomach as she listened to her parents' quarreling. In her nighttime visions, though, Dottie knew what was coming and desperately fought within herself to call out and urge her younger self to flee. Each time she failed, surrendering in exhausted terror to the scene unfolding in her mind's eye.

With the snap of a twig behind her, little Dottie's concentration on the game of marbles was broken. Before she could turn around, though, her face was pushed down onto the dusty floor and she tasted blood as an enormous weight flattened her small, slender frame. In the scene unfolding, Dottie watched her childhood self struggle and kick in vain as rough hands tugged at her floral dress and a man's bristly chin pressed into her neck, his breath sour, the pressure of his body upon hers leaving her grasping for air. She could see his black skin as his hand wrapped around her face, covering her mouth and turning her screams to muffled cries. When the pain began, she could only see the nearby stall, with her head and neck completely immobilized. The family mare's large brown eyes stared back at her in wonder, utterly without alarm. It was at this moment that Dottie, as always, woke, a scream trapped in her throat and her heart racing in terror.

She had prayed that these nightmares would cease after her marriage to Henry. Sleeping with a man she loved, she thought, would help her to feel safe. And although she found significant relief during the first few weeks of marriage—a time, she remembered, when she enjoyed Henry's companionship and, to her surprise, was pleased when he sought out lovemaking each evening—to her dismay the nightmares returned, first slowly and then as a nightly occurrence. At first, he attempted to soothe her when she awoke, yet each time her face burned with shame. That shame soon turned to rage, and within a year of marriage, she insisted that he sleep in a separate room. The two, it had been silently agreed, would never speak of her nightmares again.

Now, she pulled back her quilt, stood, and wrapped her nightgown tightly around her still thin frame. Opening the door into the hallway, she stepped into her husband's bedroom and listened for a moment to the sounds of his agitated rest, occasional snores punctuated by senseless muttering. Henry, she thought, had tried to be a good husband. But even the best man could be brought down by his sensual appetites. Only two years after their marriage, less than a year after she'd demanded Henry move to the guest room, she discovered a key in the pocket of his slacks. "The Ramada Inn," the keychain had read, and with her suspicion mounting, she had called the hotel and asked to be connected to his room. She remembered the sound of the phone ringing, her heart beating faster and faster, until a woman came onto the line. "Hello?" asked the silken voice. Dottie remained speechless until, several moments later, the woman spoke again. "Henry, is that you, honey?" Dottie slammed the receiver back into its cradle.

She never mentioned the incident to her husband. But a bitterness had taken up residence in her heart and festered there, quickly spreading and poisoning all of her affection for him. She had taken to her bed, often failing to rise in the morning and sometimes remaining there until evening when Henry, arriving home, forced her to sit with him in the living room and take a cup of soup for nourishment. It was during this time that she was first admitted to the hospital. She remembered the doctor, dressed in a white coat, his face rimmed by silver glasses, announced to both of them that she had suffered from a "nervous breakdown" and would need to be admitted for electroshock therapy. This, he insisted, was her best hope to find relief from her nerves and to return to a productive life. At the time, she had not understood what the treatment entailed.

In fact, Dottie could remember almost nothing about the procedure. Henry told her afterwards that the nurses had wheeled her away, into the bowels of the hospital, where an electric current had been shot through her brain. When she came out about an hour later, she was dazed and incoherent. For most of the following day, she hadn't even remembered her own name. Over the next few weeks, though, the procedure was repeated several times and the fog and despair that had engulfed her mind began to lift, slowly. Dottie remembered one morning in particular, when she had gotten up soon after her husband left for work and went into the kitchen. Looking out the window, she marveled at the beauty of the morning sun. Henry had remarked soon afterward that she was back to her old self, the woman he had married. The next months were the happiest in their marriage.

Although her entire life had been stricken by loneliness, over the next months she felt her isolation keenly as she longed for the company of another person, especially during the long days when her husband was at the shoe store. Though she often reflected on her husband's betrayal, the thought of leaving him never occurred to her, for that was simply not done, and so she began to think on how she might best salve her wounds. The thought of having a child came to her mind. Within days of conceiving the thought, she returned to her husband's bedroom. Although sex disgusted her still, it was a means to an end. As for Henry, he was delighted with this turn of events.

Now, she continued down the hallway and saw that Graham's bedroom door was open. Stepping inside, she saw the orderly bulletin board on the wall, its items arranged with meticulous care. He was, she reflected, a fine boy, and she felt a tenderness toward him that she had only experienced on rare occasions. She deeply regretted the path that her pregnancy and postpartum period had taken. During pregnancy, she had once again fallen into deep despair, utterly revolted by her changing, swollen body and ashamed that it was out there for the whole world to see. Soon after the birth, she had once again been admitted to the hospital, having suffered a second nervous breakdown. This time, she stayed almost two months, as she required several rounds of electroshock and ongoing monitoring before she was able to make a recovery. By the time she returned home, Hattie, the black maid, had assumed almost complete responsibility for her son's care.

For some reason, she now found herself thinking of her father, a man whom she hadn't seen in more that 20 years. The morning after the rape, he had found her face down in the barn, her dress torn and spotted with blood. Whether the man had knocked her unconscious or simply left her there whimpering, she couldn't be sure, but she could recall the feeling of the cold ground beneath her as she lay there throughout the night, drifting in and out of consciousness. Yelling with anger, her father had pried the story of the night's events from her as she sat at the kitchen table, her mother pacing back and forth in silence. Soon afterward, he had gone to the police and a manhunt was organized. Within hours, the black man was found in the woods, sleeping off a night of drinking underneath a pine tree. The hanging happened within a week and her father had insisted that she attend.

Her father had been a complicated man, she now recognized. His neck was thicker than his head, a bulging mass of soft, hanging flesh, and his stomach reached out over his belt and hung toward the ground. He had voracious appetites and was quick to anger, his already ruddy cheeks turning bright red when he became animated. After the hanging, he had sat her down on the front porch and told her she must never speak of the event again, that it would keep her from finding a husband when she was grown. Any good man, he insisted, would find her damaged if he found out what had transpired. This, she suspected, had been the beginning of the shame that had followed her throughout her life.

Dottie slowly bent over Graham's bed and gently pressed her lips to the top of her son's head, breathing in the smell of his unwashed hair. She resolved, for the first time since his birth, that she would show him the care that he deserved. Though she had feared she might destroy his innocence—as if her own ruin might somehow be infectious—she now knew that, tragically, she had deprived her son of the mother that he very much deserved.

Leaving Graham's room and making her way downstairs, she immediately felt the cold breeze from the window, open to the dark night outside. She walked to the front door and opened it. The old screen door, its screen ruptured in several places, flapped softly in the breeze, broadcasting an intermittent tapping throughout the room. She looked out into the night, considering what to do next. With no shoes readily available, she stepped outside in her bare feet, careful to hold the wrought iron railing as she navigated down into the yard, the frigid dampness of the brick steps making her shiver. Pulling her nightgown tighter still, she mustered her courage and stepped out onto the wet grass.

Against the back fence stood an old wooden shed, which had languished unused throughout Graham's childhood. The previous owners had kept chickens in that shed, but Henry had no interest in spending his evenings tending to the animals and had given them away to a farm at the edge of town. Within a few years, the shed had fallen into disrepair and, disturbed by its decaying walls and the memories it evoked of her childhood, Dottie had avoided it assiduously. Now she stood in front of it, tears forming at the corners of her eyes. Lost in her memories, she didn't hear the rustling of grass behind her. It was only when he spoke that she, startled, turned and saw Jimmy, the man she'd insisted Hattie fire earlier that day after she'd discovered that he had stolen from the family.

"You damn woman," Jimmy snarled, a bottle of bathtub gin falling from his hand and shattering on a rock in the grass, "you done ruined me! Why'd you have to go and do that? I ain't done nothing but good for you and your husband, you hear? I been tryin' to put my life a'right, getting to church every Sunday, and you've gone and ruined me!"

"What in the world are you doing out here, Jimmy?" she hissed with alarm. "You get out of here right this minute before I call Henry to chase you out with a shotgun! You're no Christian man, lurking around here with that bottle in hand."

He lurched toward her, stumbling as he navigated the uneven lawn, his lips curled in a sneer. "I'm gonna teach you somethin', lady," he snarled, as he fell forward, knocking her to the ground. As they landed, her head impacted the hard dirt, her eyes closing tightly against the pain. For several moments, Jimmy didn't move and she thought that he was unconscious. She struggled against his weight, unable to free herself. Suddenly, he reared up, roaring with rage as he wrapped his hands around her neck. Unable to scream, she struggled to breathe and, within moments, her vision began to dim. His grip was like iron, and though she clawed at his arms and face, his strength did not falter.

As the world began to fade, an image of her son flashed through her mind. Desperately she wanted to reach him, to run through the yard and up to his room, to wrap him in her arms and apologize again and again for the ways that she'd failed him. Yes, at times she had been impatient with him, even cruel. She had resented his youthful innocence because her own innocence had been destroyed so young. But this, she realized, had been unfair, a cruel repetition of all that she had suffered as a child. In a last, desperate attempt at freedom, her thumb found its way into Jimmy's eye. Feeling the soft wetness there, she pressed hard, scraping downward with her nail, gritting her teeth with effort.

He roared, louder this time, and rolled away, freeing her body from beneath his and covering his bleeding eye with both hands. She scrambled to her feet and began to run, hearing Jimmy wail behind her, his cries those of a man in unspeakable pain. Gaining speed, her mind was exhilarated by the possibility of escape and the hope that she might, against all odds, make amends. Within moments, though, she began to stumble as her bare feet scraped against the gravel scattered throughout the yard. As she approached the house's front steps, her brief hopes were shattered as she tripped once more, this time on her nightgown, its edges now ragged and filthy. With only a single moment of fear, the brick steps rushed forward, their jagged edges impacting her forehead with a loud crack. The lights inside the kitchen came to life, dimly illuminating the steps from a nearby window, and a neighbor's dog began to howl mournfully into the dark, moonless night.

TWENTY-ONE

"Killed?" she asked, her eyebrows raised in surprise. Dr. Clarice sat up straighter, took a deep breath and looked out across the room at him expectantly.

"The next morning, earlier than I usually woke up, Hattie came into my room. I remember opening my eyes and seeing her standing over me at the end of the bed, her face tight with worry. 'Graham, you have to get up now, sweetie.' Her voice was calm, even though she must have known what happened by then. I knew something was wrong. Why else would she be at our house that early in the morning?

"'What's wrong?' I asked, my heartbeat already starting to race.

"'There's been an accident, honey,' she said, sitting down on the bed next to me and putting her hand on my back. Some of the best memories of my childhood are of that hand on my back. After my mother died, Hattie stayed late, often until well past my bedtime, for a long time—months, probably. And even after that, she'd stay with me on the nights when my father didn't come home until late. After my mother's death, he'd spend his afternoons at the racetracks, gambling, before heading to the bar. But that's another story, I suppose. Anyway, I can remember her hand rubbing my back—her palms were rough, a

141

texture of skin I had never felt before—as I struggled to fall asleep. It always worked."

"It sounds like she was a tremendous comfort to you," Dr. Clarice noted.

"Yes, without a doubt. She never had children of her own. Her husband, George, and I became close as I got older. He was also kind to me. Yes, it's complicated, the racial difference and of course the fact that she technically worked for my father. But I really believe—I am sure of this—that she loved me like a child of her own. When I think of a mother's love, I think of her, not my mother."

Graham looked at the window, gazing thoughtfully into the garden. The rain had abated and drops of water made their way down the windows, weaving abstract patterns of light and color as the sun began to shine again. He wondered whether Dr. Clarice tended to the garden herself or whether it was done by the landlord. Pushing away the foreboding gathering in his chest, he spoke, determined to finish his story.

"Here's what happened, as best it was ever understood. My father heard a man wailing outside late at night and got up to see what was happening. He found my mother's bedroom door wide open and, rushing outside, found her unconscious at the bottom of our front steps, with her head bleeding. He ran back inside and called an ambulance, but my mother never recovered consciousness. I never saw her again and she died at the hospital within a few days. We don't even know what she was doing in the yard in the middle of the night. The police also found signs of a struggle in the yard and lots of blood in one spot. That was the beginning of a police search that took at least a few days. Finally they found out—I don't know how—that it was our yard man, Jimmy, who had assaulted her. She had injured him, gouged out his eye, and while running back toward the house, she tripped and hit her head on the front steps. She almost got away."

"Oh, my," Dr. Clarice murmured, "that's quite disturbing."

"Yes," he replied. "Now, Hattie kept most of the details from me as they unfolded and my father was simply beside himself with grief and didn't communicate much at all. It was summer, so I wasn't in school. I'm sure if I had been, there would have been a lot of gossip about it. As I grew older, I learned that the man, Jimmy, got the electric chair within a few months, after a brief trial in which my father testified. Jimmy claimed he didn't remember the assault until the end of his life—he was drunk, apparently, so that may be true—but he did say that my mother had fired him for made up reasons earlier that day. Hattie confirmed the truth of this for me a few years before she died."

"There is so much for us to talk about here—it's such a traumatic and complex episode—and given our limited time, we'll need to come back to it in future sessions. But for today, tell me: what does it bring up for you, to talk with me about this?"

"I don't feel as much as I think I should, to be honest. It's something that I grew up finding out about in bits and pieces, and I've thought about it a lot. But maybe I don't want to feel much, like you suggested earlier, It is a horrific episode, isn't it?"

"Horrific is, I think, an entirely appropriate word. You know, it's striking that you lost your mother at such a young age and in such a traumatic way and, since then, have had trouble forming romantic relationships with women. Besides what we've been talking about with respect to aggression, I wonder whether becoming interested in a woman brings up anxiety about loss. That you'll get closer to a woman and then lose her, the person you've come to value, perhaps even in a horrible and traumatic fashion."

He considered this for a moment. "That's possible," he said, "but I have to admit that I've never thought of the two things as connected before. I'll have to give it a lot of reflection. Maybe we can talk about it more next time."

"We *are* almost out of time for today," she affirmed, "and I want to leave a few moments to discuss how, or if, you'd like to move forward with this process."

"I've felt comfortable with you today." he replied. "You've been easy to talk to and I actually had no idea that there would be so much to say about a single day in my life. It's been a relief to speak so freely, because I haven't spoken about it to anyone before, really. Actually, the idea of stopping for today makes me sad but also a little anxious, a strange combination. I don't know why."

"It's a loss, even if only until we are able to meet again."

"Yes, that's true," he replied thoughtfully. "I did want to ask you for your opinion. Do you think you can be helpful to me? Does this seem like a good fit between psychoanalyst and patient, between you and me?"

"I do feel hopeful," she nodded, "and I would certainly like for us to continue our conversation, to learn more about how we can best work together. I think we've made a good start today but there is much more to discuss."

Graham looked down at his hands crossed in his lap. Sitting silently for several moments, a troubled look gathered on his typically neutral face.

"You look worried."

"I feel apprehensive. When you said that—that you would like for us to meet again—my heart started beating harder and I had an image of myself running out of the room. It's so confusing because I didn't want the session to end. That you'd like to meet again is exactly what I wanted to hear or, maybe I should say, what I *thought* I wanted to hear. Now I suspect it's more complex, right?"

"I've just said that I was interested in us becoming closer, so to speak, as analyst and patient in our work together; that I think we might form a relationship that could be deeply meaningful and could bring you some relief."

"You're saying it's the same anxiety that I experience with these women I've dated." he said, a look of surprised interest on his face. "The anxiety that, perhaps, stems from the early loss of my mother, among other things."

"I think that's a possibility worth taking seriously."

"That idea brings me some relief. It gives me some distance from the feeling and makes me think it might be possible for it to change."

"Yes, I think we're starting to understand something important here," she replied, "but we do have to stop for today."

After a brief conversation in which they determined that meetings would occur twice weekly on regular days and times, Dr. Clarice stood and walked to the door. Opening it, she gestured for Graham to step outside. As he nodded goodbye, an unfamiliar feeling grew inside him. Yes, he was certainly apprehensive about what he had just committed to—meeting twice each week with this woman who had a remarkable ability to help him understand his own mind, but who also demanded that he think about a painful and disappointing history. He also felt a familiar dread, stemming, he suspected, from the possibility that the treatment might not help after all. But alongside the fear lived a hopeful excitement, a kind of vitality that he hadn't felt in many years, if ever.

As Graham walked toward the door, he noticed a desk, tucked in a corner of the office that he hadn't been able to see while he was sitting in his chair. A pale wooden structure, it was unadorned save for a large, black calendar covered in red and black ink, and a small photograph. Not wanting to intrude, he resisted the impulse to investigate the photograph directly, instead taking it in from the corner of his eye. As best he could tell, it depicted a single tombstone covered in red and purple flowers, surrounded by green grass. Before he could determine whether his interpretation of the image had been accurate, he passed Dr. Clarice and was outside her office, walking down the hallway.

He continued down the hall through which he had entered almost an hour before. In that hour, he had reflected on his history in a way that was entirely new to him and that made sense of his suffering. On the one hand, he felt the weight of the difficulties that he had endured—the burdens he had carried his entire life yet, strangely, without being entirely aware that he was so weighed down by them. On the other, he felt, in his relationship with Dr. Clarice, dimly aware of possibilities—for himself and for his relationships with others—that he had never before encountered. This, above all, gave him hope for a different future and a motivation to continue on the journey they had begun.

As he stepped out on to the sidewalk, Graham saw that the sun above him had brightened. Its rays reflected almost painfully from the puddles scattered across the concrete. Less than a block away, a mother and child, the latter maybe five or six years old, walked together, holding hands, the child talking excitedly and skipping from time to time. He smiled wistfully at them, a melancholy feeling accompanying the nearly undetectable tears in his eyes, and headed toward his car to begin the evening's journey home.

AFTERWORD

Dr. Clarice stood in her office, now empty, her workday at its end. As she gently stretched her back, which cried out from a long day of sitting, she reflected on what had just transpired with her new patient. The two of them had made a good start and, if fortune were on their side, they might engage in a long, productive psychoanalysis. She felt, she now realized, an unusually strong connection to him. Yes, she imagined that her son, had he survived, might have been like Graham, a young man of striking intelligence and deep feeling. Her fantasy surprised her, for she had rarely allowed herself to imagine what might have been had her son survived, for fear that train of thought would lead to unbearable pain. But while the idea evoked that old grief, it also brought her hope. Perhaps she would be able to help Graham set his life on a better path. Though she knew it was irrational, it felt as if this might, in some small way, redeem the loss of her son.

Dr. Clarice turned off the lights in her office and locked the door, promising herself that she would water her plants tomorrow. Several other clinicians in her suite were still working, so she left the front door unlocked as she left the building. Outside, the ground was wet with rain that had fallen throughout the day and she appreciated the shimmer of the afternoon sun as it reflected on the pavement. She paused in front of the bookstore next to her office, gazing absently into the display window, to see several postcards decorated with letterpress animal designs. One in particular caught her eye: a hawk standing atop a branch, gazing down at its baby, which she vaguely remembered was called an *eyas*, in its nest.

Crossing the street, she thought again of Donald Winnicott, the British pediatrician turned psychoanalyst who had been a major inspiration during her training. His theory, a reflection of his personality, emphasized the importance of play in emotional health. She had read that he often rode his bicycle through London, dressed in a formal suit, his feet on the handlebars. Naturally, this scandalized his buttoned-up contemporaries. She thought of his paper, *Fear of Breakdown*, written in the last year of his life and published in 1974, three years after his abrupt death. In it, he suggested that patients who fear a catastrophic event in the future —an event that would lead them to fall apart—are actually struggling to metabolize a breakdown that already happened in their early lives, during a time when such intense feelings simply could not be assimilated.

She wondered what Graham's early life had been like. Today he had voiced his fear that something terrible would befall him, something emotionally unbearable. She also learned that his mother had been hospitalized soon after his birth. What had that separation been like for him? Infants, after all, are utterly dependent upon their caretakers to soothe their emotional distress. Had Hattie been available after his mother's hospitalization to comfort him? If not, how upset had he become and how often? They might never find exact answers to these questions, but in time, feelings would emerge, both from him and between the two of them, that would point them in the right direction.

Yes, in time they would have a sense of what it had been like for him as a young child.

As Dr. Clarice approached her car, without thinking she pulled out her cellphone and dialed her husband. Her second marriage had been far more successful than her first. Her husband, a prominent academic, was a kind, thoughtful man who had also been married before and fathered two children, both now young adults. The two met in their 40s, both having grappled with life's challenges and, slowly, they had fallen in love. Now, though they each had full lives of their own, they remained steadfastly connected, each a stillpoint for the other as they grew older together. Yet she often felt that their marriage had grown routinized, a comfortable but familiar give-and-take. Tonight, to her surprise, she decided to invite him to go salsa dancing. Who knew, after all, how much time they had left?

Meanwhile, as Graham climbed into his blue hatchback to drive home, his mind worked to digest the session. He did not see Dr. Clarice, merely a block away, as she got into her green sedan and pulled out into traffic. It took all of his energy to assimilate what he felt had been one of the most productive encounters of his adult life, a meeting in which he had been forced to reflect on his childhood to an extent that he had avoided so far, largely because of the emotional pain evoked by remembering. And yet he found that, when accompanied by Dr. Clarice, these explorations yielded more than just pain. They also provided hope that something new, even transformative, might emerge; that the deadening and fruitless repetitions of the past might be laid to rest.

As he drove, he wondered about the picture of the tombstone that sat on Dr. Clarice's desk. Who had she lost and how long ago? Was she grieving even now? The thought unexpectedly made him tearful. Why, he wondered, was he so moved by this conjecture? After all, he had only spoken to this woman for the first time today, and only for an hour. Pausing in his thoughts to regain his equilibrium, his mind drifted back to that time, many years ago, that he stood in the freezing rain through his mother's funeral. He remembered his father's face, still stricken from finding his wife's injured body less than a week ago, as he stood before the preacher, who spoke about love and loss and the good Lord who was waiting for all of us at the end of our journeys. Graham had not cried on that day; and even now he remembered feeling apart from those in mourning, from his father.

When the funeral ended, he stood beside his father as each guest approached, mostly members of the family's church, each expressed kindness and concern. He found the experience overwhelming, though he was moved that so many members of the community had attended in spite of the rain and cold. For the most part, it was the wives that spoke, their husbands standing by in mute support. His father, drawing on a well of strength deep inside himself, greeted each guest by name and thanked them for attending. Today, Graham remembered almost nothing of what had been said or who had said it, save for a single woman who had approached them, alone, her dangling earrings framing an otherwise plain face, unremarkable brown hair falling in curls to her shoulders.

"People don't dress for funerals the way they used to, and that's a shame," she began, to the surprise of Graham and his father. "Well, I am sorry for your loss. I knew Dottie when she was young, yeah? She was my best friend in grade school. We had a falling out soon after and we ain't talked much since then, but she's always had a spot in my heart."

"Is that right, ma'am?" Henry asked.

"Yes, sir, it sure is. Well, I won't take up much of your time, but let me just tell you a story or two that I remember, because otherwise I don't think you'll be hearin' them, now that she's breathed her last." The guests standing behind her in line shifted uncomfortably, each huddling under an umbrella to escape the cold rain. "Well, when I was just in the first grade, my momma dropped me off and I was nervous as a cat in a room full o' rockin' chairs. Didn't know a single soul in that old school and our teacher, Mrs. Needle, well she was mean as a snake. Here I am, 'bout to piss my britches, and who comes over but Dottie. Sits down next to me, asks 'bout this or that, I don't remember, but sets me right at ease. That's what a good soul she was, you hear? We were fast friends then on, that's certain."

"Oh," Henry said, uncertain how to respond. After an awkward silence, he continued. "I appreciate you taking the time to share that with us. She did have a good heart."

"That's the truth," the woman affirmed, her earrings shaking as she nodded vigorously. "Whatever reason, I don't know, but 'round the fourth grade, she became a different person. Didn't speak to nobody no more, not even me. I always thought somethin' must've happened in her home, but I don't know what that might be. Well, we didn't speak much after that. I wish we'd mended our fences before now."

"I know," Henry affirmed, "that she appreciates you coming today."

The woman stepped aside and allowed other guests to approach. How much time passed, Graham wasn't sure, but finally the guests began to depart and the rain slackened before ceasing entirely. His father went to speak with the preacher, to offer his thanks for the service. As Graham stood waiting for his father to finish, the sun came out, warming his frozen hands. He heard the sound of footsteps behind him.

Turning, he saw George, Hattie's husband, standing before him No matter how long he lived, he was certain he would always retain that image: a six-foot-tall black man in a deep purple suit, holding a gold tipped cane that, Graham realized in retrospect, was purely decorative. The afternoon sun illuminated George's well-oiled beard, still entirely black, and though his face had been carved by time, his sad smile communicated a depth of fellow feeling that Graham had not encountered in any of the other guests.

"Graham," George said, his voice gruff but warm, "let's walk together."

Graham began to walk away from the cemetery and down a long, winding path leading back to the main road. When George caught up with him, he reached out to rest one hand on Graham's shoulder while the other held his ornamental cane, which tapped the gravel with each step the pair took. For several moments, they walked together in silence. Graham could smell his cologne, a sweet yet masculine smell that seemed entirely unique to him.

"Son," he said, "you've come on tryin' times. I'm sorry for your loss."

"Thank you," Graham replied softly. He appreciated the sincerity in George's voice. The man seemed to understand his pain in a way the white folks hadn't.

"Yes, son," George continued, "all we can do is turn to the Lord. What we know for sure is that your momma, well, she's up restin' in Heaven with Jesus. Do you understand, son?"

He understood. He appreciated George's kindness yet, at the same time, regretted that he did not share his confidence in his mother's fate. Even before her death, Graham had doubted the reality of the Heaven that everyone he knew talked about so often. That doubt had driven a wedge between him and those around him, leaving him feeling apart from them; even from his own father and from Hattie, both of whom were believers. Now, he despaired that he could not join George in his faith.

"That man, Jimmy," George continued, "Well, he was like Legion. Do you understand what I mean here, son? Do you know the story 'bout Legion?"

Noticing the puzzled look on Graham's face, George continued to speak, his voice becoming more excited as he went on.

"In the Good Book, in the chapter of Luke, there's a story that comes to mind. When Jesus sailed to the country of Gerasenes—which was direct across from Galilee, you see—when he got off that boat, he saw a man afflicted with demons. The man didn't wear no clothes—none at'all—and he lived up in them tombs, amongst all the spirits and ghosts and such. When Jesus asked the man for his name, he replied, 'Legion.' What he meant, you see, is that there were all sorts of demons living inside him—a whole bunch of 'em."

Graham looked at him, uncertain how to reply.

"Now you see why I said Jimmy was like Legion, yeah? There was a legion of demons in that afflicted man, same as with poor ole' Jimmy."

Graham nodded, understanding now that George meant that Jimmy had been possessed by demons and that, for him, this explained why Jimmy had murdered Graham's mother. Of this, he was even more skeptical than of his mother's Heavenly rest. Although he knew that many black Christians believed in demons and other supernatural phenomena—speaking in tongues being the most extreme example he'd encountered—his family had attended a church that didn't emphasize these aspects of the faith, even regarding them with suspicion. More likely, Jimmy had been angry with his mother and drunk on alcohol besides and, knowing Dottie, he might have had good reason to hold a grudge against her.

"So, on that day," George continued, his voice reaching an intimidating intensity. His eyes were afire with enthusiasm and as he spoke, bits of spittle flew from the sides of his mouth. "On that day, there was a whole lot of pigs eatin' grass on the hillside and Jesus cast those demons out of the man and into them pigs, which soon ran headlong down that hill and into the lake, where they drowned. That man, he was free of them demons, you see? He got dressed, found his right mind, and sat at the feet of Jesus."

Graham nodded in an effort to show appreciation for the man's efforts, though secretly his heart remained unmoved by his words. He felt even more apart than before.

"What I'm saying, son," George said, his voice returning to its normal volume as he concluded his story, "is that only the Lord can help Jimmy. This whole, terrible situation, we have to give it to the Lord, 'cause it's out of our hands now."

Even today, Graham could remember how his heart had fallen as George continued to speak. This kind, decent man was trying to set his heart at ease, but Graham was impervious to his efforts. For the first time in his life, he realized that he was completely outside of the faith in which he had been raised. The edifice of his religious belief, previously fissured, now shattered, never to be made right again. Though he didn't know it at the time, he would spend the next few decades trying to make sense of a world that had been rendered insensible by this loss. This, finally, lead him to study philosophy and, then, to Dr. Clarice's office to understand, and hopefully to heal, his mind.

Returning from his thoughts, Graham sighed. He opened the door to his apartment and stepped inside. He had several hundred pages to read that evening, assignments that he had put off until the last minute to complete. Well, he loved reading and looked forward to the task. As he took a seat in his favorite chair, he noticed the small, wooden train sitting on the bookshelf across the room. Its red and blue paint was faded and chipped with time but the memento had followed him to college and then in his move across the country for graduate school. As he gazed at the train, he remembered Hattie fondly. He remembered, above all, the feeling of her hands, rough and kind, as she rubbed his back while he fell asleep.

As the moments passed, his mind turned, once again, to Charlotte. He had thought of her often over the years, but each time an image of her arose in his mind unbidden, he tried to banish it, tormented by the blend of longing and fear that accompanied his memory. Now, he thought for the first time that he might call her, even if only to apologize once again for failing her. His fears were like mirages that tortured a man thirsting in the desert, constructions of his own mind that, in time and with hard work in his psychoanalysis, he might be able to change. Yes, there was hope.

He took out his cellphone and, looking down at its screen, pulled up Charlotte's number. It had languished among his notes, which he had recently digitized, for years. His thumb hovered above the number, only a mere tap needed to initiate the call. After several moments, he clicked the phone off and returned it to his pocket. He would call Charlotte. But he would see Dr. Clarice again soon and wanted to talk the matter over with her first. Yes, he would see Dr. Clarice again soon, though not as soon as he would have liked.

www.ingramcontent.com/pod-product-compliance
Lightning Source LLC
Chambersburg PA
CBHW071013180726
48291CB00004B/1445